Will Nathaniel Harben, Richard Hooker Wilmer

A Mute Confessor

The Romance of a Southern Town

Will Nathaniel Harben, Richard Hooker Wilmer

A Mute Confessor
The Romance of a Southern Town

ISBN/EAN: 9783337347871

Printed in Europe, USA, Canada, Australia, Japan

Cover: Foto ©Andreas Hilbeck / pixelio.de

More available books at **www.hansebooks.com**

A MUTE CONFESSOR:

THE

ROMANCE OF A SOUTHERN TOWN.

A Novel

BY

WILLIAM N. HARBEN,

Author of " White Marie," " Almost Persuaded."

BOSTON, MASS.:

Arena Publishing Company,

COPLEY SQUARE,

1892.

TO MY SISTER GEORGIE.

A MUTE CONFESSOR.

CHAPTER I.

AMONG Edgar Morton's acquaintances it went without saying that he had marked peculiarities. Some of his most intimate friends admitted that there were times when, failing to fathom his fitful moods, they felt uncomfortable in his company.

He was young, handsome, tall, and had a commanding figure. His high, broad forehead was indicative of a lofty and poetic intellect. His eyes and hair were very dark, his features as clear-cut as a cameo. People were rarely free with him, for he was exceedingly reserved.

"Egad!" once said a noted politician, who figured extensively in New York society and had met Edgar several times at the "Authors' Club"

—" egad, that young fellow is as reserved as the North Pole ; but mind my words, he'll come to the front one of these days ! He has just enough of the mysterious about him to make him take. He knows when to hold his tongue; when he is not thoroughly posted he is as mute as a clam ; but where he knows his ground he is as impregnable as a stone wall. The consequence is that when he *does* express an opinion people listen to him."

From a small town in Massachusetts Morton had come to the metropolis to gratify a yearning, insatiable ambition to make a name for himself. He was well educated and well read, and had begun his career in New York as a general writer for newspapers. His editors, who were acquainted with all he wrote anonymously, as well as over his own name, agreed that his work was marvellously clever. They went so far as to say that he showed rare and deep insight into human nature, that now and then he rose to beautiful heights of poetic fancy.

These editors were less surprised than many others when a leading publisher announced a novel by him, and not a few of his admirers watched for its appearance with sharply whetted curiosity.

"Transgression," met with almost unprecedented favor for a "first book." Critics prophesied that, with time and experience, the author would acquire considerable and enduring fame; his imagery, his art, his pathos, his dainty touches of humor, were divine gifts.

Morton opened his eyes in a new and charming world; he suddenly heard himself mentioned far and near as one of the kindling lights of American literature upon which the breath of public admiration was steadily blowing. He was sought by the wealthy and by the great. His peculiarities, once deplored, were now regarded as the royal offspring of imperial genius.

Despite all the *furore* he had raised, Morton, be it said to his credit, in his secret soul despised himself for weaknesses not dreamed of by the public. He had always harbored a belief, born, perhaps, of his exalted ideas of truth and art,—and it sometimes amounted to a fear that almost staggered him,—that he could never become truly great till he was purer of soul than he really was. His chief faults were affectation and deceit. His mother, who had died years before, had often said to him :

"You have one serious fault, Edgar, and I am afraid you will have to struggle against it all your life. You are very rarely your true self; you often employ deceit to gain a point which could more easily be gained through candor and honesty."

Like many another man of Napoleonic aspirations and nervous temperament, Morton's pride was often galled by contact with obstacles which, despite all his cleverness, he could not surmount. Lack of sufficient means to gratify naturally extravagant tastes was the greatest barrier to his content. He had genius, but he had vanity. His fame and popularity drew him into social circles where he could ill afford to stay, and an indomitable pride held him there. His earnings were meagre compared with the incomes of his associates. Their money flowed as freely as water, but he was obliged to stint himself, and to stifle many desires in order to keep up appearances. In the summer, when his friends left the city for fashionable resorts or to make trips to Europe, Morton could not afford to go ; so he pretended to be pressed with duties, and remained in heated New York to nurse his discontent and bewail his ill-luck.

It was this combination of circumstances that made him first think of bettering his condition by marriage. Miss Jean Wharton, the orphaned heiress of a superb fortune, whom he had met frequently at her uncle's fashionable home in West Fifty-eighth Street, began to show a strong liking for him. He visited her frequently, and almost before he realized the fact they were engaged.

Morton had never felt even the faintest thrill of real love for Miss Wharton, and there were moments in which his better self did stern battle with the alluring temptation to wed her. At such times he would almost resolve to break off with the heiress and be true to himself, but the appearance of an urgent bill collector and the sight of his empty purse usually made him desperate, and caused him to think with grim satisfaction upon a certain unannounced social event, and to draw mind-pictures of an Eden where the fiend, Poverty, did not kill genius in the bud. He used to soliloquize over the matter something like this :

" Well, what if my whole soul is not absolutely bound up in the girl ?   What if I do
not dream about her, and think her a veritable
paragon of human loveliness and virtue ? she
can help me out of a beastly mire where I
don't belong.   She takes to me because I am
a little out of her run.   I can give her all she
wants, and she can supply me with what I
must have, or be a slave all my days.   I have
never loved anybody with the raging confla-
gration of the heart that poets rave about, and
perhaps I never should, even if I remained
unmarried into frosty old bachelorhood."

CHAPTER II.

THE gas was shedding a mellow light through the pink and pale-blue globes in the drawing-room of a brown-stone mansion in West Fifty-eighth Street. The furniture, the statues of bronze and marble, the bric-à-brac, the paintings, the unique screens were scattered here and there with that seeming disorder which is highest art. In a luxurious arm-chair, upholstered in soft brown leather, Miss Jean Wharton sat awaiting Edgar Morton. There was a characteristic ring—one impetuous jerk of the bell-pull. A faint flush struggled into the young woman's cheeks, and she rose tremulously to greet her visitor.

She was far from handsome; she could scarcely lay claim to one redeeming feature. She looked the typical old maid. Footprints of the proverbial crow were visible in the facial sands

about her gray, lack-lustre eyes, where that
heartless, tell-tale bird had been stalking about
for thirty years, taking zealous care that the
frequent tides of cosmetics should not obliterate
his tracks. To Morton's fastidious eyes she
was too tall, too scrawny; her hair lacked gloss,
her eyes vivacity.

He smiled according to habit when he entered,
and took her outstretched hand. With her
he was less reserved than with the rest of his
friends, else he could not have won her regard.

"I am so glad you came," she said, when
he had seated himself; "you have neglected
me very much of late."

"I have been very busy, my dear," said he,
hoping that she had not noticed his name in
the society papers as being present at several
receptions he had attended since he had seen
her. "I have an awful lot of work to do.
You know that in order to exist, a poor, moneyless toiler like myself must utilize every spare
moment; but, of course, you can't understand
—in your position."

She sighed and put her costly lace handkerchief up to her face.

"But it will not be so always," said she, her

blushes deepening; "some time you will allow those who love you to help you."

A look of mingled shame and embarrassment flitted across the author's handsome visage. He rose, ostensibly to replace a photograph which had fallen from a table, and yawned a little in secret as he passed behind her chair. Her eyes followed his movements wistfully, her face wore an expression of blended tenderness and admiration.

"A poor beggar, such as I am, has no right to marry a wealthy woman," said he, standing behind her and turning the leaves of an album on the table. He had assumed a little air and tone of despondency, knowing by past experience how such tricks roused her sympathies. He heartily despised himself for his duplicity as he went on : "What will the world say of the wealthy Miss Wharton throwing herself away upon a humble bohemian ? "

"You promised you would not talk that way any more," said she, visibly pained. "What do I care ? What should you care what idle gossips may say ? No other man but you would give such things a thought. But I suppose it is part of your sensitive nature. I admit that I might have suspected the motives of any other suitor, but you are so different from the rest of your sex. I feel honored that you—a man of your refinement of nature and tastes, should fancy poor me. I am so insignificant. I was just thinking the other day that I should be, oh! such a poor companion for you. You will have to love me a great deal to overlook my shortcomings. Tell me really what you first saw in me to attract you. I am not good-looking, I am not good."

She had made that request of him before, and he had found that it required much skill to meet it gracefully. He had firmly made up his mind to marry her, and yet she was at times almost repulsive to him, more so in her present affectionate mood than ever. He had shuddered hundreds of times over the thought that she was to be his wife.

He sighed audibly, and going to her chair, bent over her with well-assumed feeling in his mien.

"What did I see in you?"—his dreamily-spoken words seemed to exude from a heart surcharged with love; but even then he shuddered as he looked down upon her flabby cheek, upon which grew short, white hairs magnified by the oblique rays of the gaslight. He put his soft, tapering hand about her neck, feeling a peculiar creeping sensation at the roots of his hair. "What did I see in you?" he repeated, slowly, as if he had seen so much in her that he was at a loss for words to express it. "Why do you ask?"

He was too artistic in all things to attempt to flatter her by itemizing charms she did not possess, by praising her hair, her eyes, her form. From his knowledge of her credulity he knew that he could please her more in another way. When he spoke, his eyes abetted his voice:

"To tell you the truth, Jean, I do not comprehend it. No mortal can comprehend love; it is as mysterious and as divine as space. I only know that I felt drawn to you" (and this was truth) "as I was never drawn to a woman before."

Her face was aglow. He regretted that he had expressed so much, for it made her roll her eyes up towards him till their sclerotic coats were unbecomingly exposed.

"I am so happy to-night!"

She caught his hand in her thin fingers and drew it down over her shoulder to her lips. Then she threw her head back and looked up into his face. She wanted him to kiss her; she thought he did not do so because he was timid, because he was contrasting in his mind her wealth and his poverty. He read her thoughts, and essayed to don the garment she had made for him, for he did not want to comply with her desire.

"Why don't you kiss me?" she asked. "Edgar, I really believe you are afraid of me."

He smiled. A cool mist seemed to enshroud his brain, and condense itself and trickle down his spine as he bent and kissed her. A moment later he was angered with himself. Why was he such a villain? Why had Fate tempted him to play such a disgusting, humiliating part? He wanted her millions because they were necessary to his cherished plans of future greatness, but the price to be paid for them assumed horrible proportions at times.

"You wrote me you had something important to confide to me," she went on softly, when he had resumed his chair.

She had thrust a long, slender foot from be-

neath her skirts.   At the sight of it he felt a
thrill of repugnance run over him.   He had
never liked the shape of her foot ; he had frequently thought it very inartistic.   The ball
was too prominent, the foot itself too flat, too
long.

"I am going away for a few weeks," was
his answer.

She started, and a pallor ran into her face.

" Going away ? "

"Yes ; I have finished all the work I have
here at present.   I have for some time thought
I should lay the scene of a romance in the
South.   To do it I shall have to spend a few
weeks among the people there.   I shall find
it hard to be away from you—from all my
friends, of course—but I feel that I must go."

" You always think of your duty," she said,
gently ; " I admire you for it ; but I wish it
called you here instead of there.

" When do you go ? " she ventured, after a
moment's silence.

"Two weeks from to-day.   And I had almost
forgotten, Jean ; you know that about everything an author does or contemplates doing is
made public.   I do not want any one to know
2

what I have in view, nor where I am. In order to accomplish this I shall be obliged to assume another name. I want to be thrown among the Southern people to study their characteristics, their customs ; if they knew me to be an author they would be on their guard. Mr. Lang, of my publishing firm, is the only one besides yourself who will have my secret. He will attend to forwarding my mail."

She smiled gratefully.

"How strange !" she said. "I am so glad you confided in me. You know no one can get it from me. Edgar, I feel very proud of you and your work. You have heard me mention the Saxons, uncle's rich friends. They were here to dinner last night. Somehow your name came up at the table, and Mrs. Saxon said, ' Why, you don't say Edgar Morton visits you !' Even uncle was proud to tell her that you came here frequently. Mrs. Saxon ran on for quite a time in a most enthusiastic strain about what she had heard of you and your literary work, and after dinner she asked me if I could show her your handwriting. Of course, I did not want her to read any of your notes, so I let her see the pretty copy of 'Transgression' in which you wrote that beautiful verse. You should have seen how much she admired it. She said that we ought to feel honored to have you for a friend. Can you wonder that I do, and that I love you and feel flattered by your love?"

He smiled indifferently.

"She is very kind. We writers have a hard time, but we are amply rewarded when we are appreciated. I have accomplished nothing so far. I hope to do something worth leaving behind me, but I have hardly made a beginning yet."

"How strange that you should care for anything of that kind!" said she, venturing to lay her thin, bejewelled hand upon his as it rested on the arm of his chair. "I can't imagine myself feeling an interest in anything which is to be read by people after my death. I care little for any books but yours, anyway."

His pulse did not beat a whit more quickly at feeling her touch. He looked into her wizen face critically, reflectively, wondering if, after all, he could afford to barter his freedom for her fortune—if he could ever think of her as a man should think of his wife.

"You have not told me," she went on, as he

stood at the door, ready to bid her good-night, "what your new name will be during your voluntary exile."

"Mr. Lang has re-christened me; he has given me the name of his grandfather, Marshal Dudley. I feel as if I had a right to use it, since I have his permission."

"Oh, it is so pretty, but not so pretty as——"

He interrupted her with a light kiss on her forehead, and turned away. The cool air outside was refreshing, and he inhaled it with a relish.

"At any rate," he said to himself, as he walked along slowly, "I shall have to see her but once more before I go, and then—rest—rest, for awhile at least."

CHAPTER III.

IT was a balmy morning in July when Edgar Morton arrived in Chattanooga, Tennessee. He had heard so much of Lookout Mountain that he could not resist the temptation to stay a few days at one of the hotels on its summit.

He alighted from a sleeping-car in the "car-shed," as the inhabitants termed the large union passenger depot in the centre of the city. As he was emerging from the station, satchel in hand, a score of negroes met him.

"Ca'ge, boss? Yer 'tis, suh; any part de city for twenty-five cents!" urged one, as he snatched at the satchel eagerly.

"Dis way, boss! mine ride yer ez easy ez er cradle!" pleaded another, bowing servilely, whip and hat in hand.

"Palace Hotel! Reed House! Stanton

Hotel!" bawled half-a-dozen black hotel-run-
ners, as they gathered around him.

Morton was a little bewildered by their eagerness and their characteristic visages, but he did
not release his satchel.

"I am going to the Mountain," he said.

He had no sooner spoken than the crowd left
him, and ran pell-mell after more profitable
passengers.

"You kin go up de broad-gauge track, ur
tek de incline plane, whichever yer lak, suh,"
said a colored bootblack, politely, who was
rolling up a scrap of carpet and putting it in
his blacking-holder. "Ef yer go up de broad-
gauge, yer kin tek de train in dis shed in 'bout
twenty minutes; but ef you'd ruther go de
incline, all yer gotter do is ter tek de 'lectric
cyar out deh in de street, en fus' thing you
know, you at de incline."

"What is the best hotel up there?" Edgar
asked.

"De 'Inn,' suh; hit des built, en de biges'
house in de Newnited States, so I year um all
say. Fum de tower on de top yer kin see inter
seben diffunt States."

Having decided to take the incline he

boarded a street car and was soon sailing through
the suburbs, toward a great cone-shaped mass
of earth and stone which towered high into the
shimmering, sun-lighted clouds. Morton was
beginning to enjoy his trip heartily, and was
better satisfied with himself than he had been
for years. He was fond of adventure, and its
spirit seemed constantly hovering over him.

In a few minutes he reached the station of
the incline railway. The car was open at the
sides and at the end facing the foot of the
mountain, so as to enable passengers to behold
the grand view as they ascended into the clouds.

He looked up the sheer, rugged mountain-
side in awe. The winding track, with its hum-
ming cable, made its tortuous way among jut-
ting bowlders and cliffs, and over frightful
chasms, on frail-looking trestles.

"How far is it to the top?" Edgar heard a
man ask.

"It's almost a mile," was the reply, "but
we make it in less than seven minutes."

"All ready!" said the conductor, and he
pressed his thumb upon an electric button.
There was a tinkling of a bell, and a sonorous,
double-toned whistle from the engine-house

near by, and the car began to move. To Morton's eye the earth seemed to be sliding from beneath him. The car increased its speed. Every passenger seemed spellbound. Morton felt a cool, vacant sensation in his breast. This feeling gradually gave way to intense and poetic enjoyment as the broad landscape opened out before his sight. Down, down sank the earth; up, up went the car, as if borne upon the wings of the balmy air into the ambient clouds.

The view constantly widened in all directions. Toward the left lay the Tennessee river, winding like a serpent through a landscape checked with farms and forests and dotted with farmhouses. Beyond the river lay Chattanooga, in mingled haze and smoke, her buildings looking as flat as if they were drawn on a map.

At length the car stopped at a broad, flat plateau. From that point the view was sublime, and Morton sat down upon a bench, beneath a blue-and-white striped canopy, to wait for the hotel train to start.

"All aboard!" shouted a conductor, and the little engine was soon tugging and steaming over the rock-bound track along the brow of the mountain.

There was something in the appearance of
the long hotel, with its towers, its broad, never-
ending balconies, and its luxury of space, that
charmed Morton. It was about ten o'clock
when he arrived, and the verandas, the reading-
room, and the parlors were thronged with guests.
Some were promenading, some engaged in playing cards, others were reading and writing,
while an orchestra was playing in an alcove in
the spacious office.

"Marshal Dudley, Boston," was the signature
Morton wrote upon the register.

He bit his lip to hide a smile when the clerk
asked: "Mr. Dudley, do you wish to go to
your room at once?"

In less than an hour Morton had refreshed
himself with a bath, had dressed himself in a
becoming light-gray suit, and was rather impa-
tient to be below among the pleasure-seekers.
The strains of music which faintly reached his
ears were enticing. He surveyed himself in a
mirror, and as he noted how perfectly his clothes
fitted his statuesque figure and how much his curl-
ing mustache became his well-carved features,
he was satisfied with his personal appearance.

The other guests evidently agreed with the

masquerading author, for when he was sauntering through the halls and balconies, enjoying
a fragrant cigar, many a female glance rested
on him, and many a bright eye in the group of
ladies in the office looked stealthily over the
register to ascertain his name.

"Marshal Dudley; what a charming name!"
remarked Miss De Witt, a pretty Georgian
belle, to a cluster of speculating damsels; "he
looks like an actor, or an artist."

"I venture he is a lawyer," said a pretty
girl from Virginia. "Any one can see that he
is intellectual. Boston men are usually so, you
know."

Morton was too close an observer not to
notice that he attracted attention, but was far
too sensible to appear conscious of it. He
bought a morning paper and took a seat out on
the balcony, pretending to be absorbed in reading, while taking note of everything around.
He was struck with the gentle, refined beauty of
the women, and the polite bearing of the men.

Presently, amid a throng of promenaders,
he caught a glimpse of the most beautiful girl
he had ever seen. She had a pair of great, indescribable brown eyes, and a mass of golden hair.

She was tall, lithe, and had a perfect figure.
She was leaning on the arm of an old gray-
headed man, and walked past Morton's chair
with the ease and freedom of a young goddess.
She wore a gown of some soft, clinging stuff,
of a peculiar shade of brown, slightly lighter
than her eyes, with dainty bits of turquoise-
blue peeping here and there. In the cast of
her well-chiselled face there was a something
which bespoke remarkable powers of intellect.
Her wonderful eyes, veiled with sweeping lashes,
seemed to breathe ideality ; her every undulant
motion to awake a sleeping charm.

Edgar's heart bounded ; a thrill ran through
his every fibre. The couple passed on. He
rose, tossed his cigar over the balustrade, and
followed them.

"Papa dear," he overheard her say—and the
melody of her voice thrilled him strangely,—
"you are too much troubled. Throw it off ;
mamma is better now ; this air will do her
good."

"I should be altogether lost without you,
darling——" sighed the parent ; but a sudden
gust of wind bore the rest of the sentence
away from Morton's ears.

As they paused at the edge of the balcony to look at the scenery, Edgar passed them, and walked to the end of the building, and then, turning back, he found them seated together on a rustic bench. The girl held a newspaper from which she was reading aloud in a softly modulated tone. As she leaned her elbows on the old man's knees, and bent her head over the paper, there was, in her softened posture, an ineffable something that appealed to the author's highest sense of the pure and beautiful. At a glance he remarked the exquisite formation of her white, tapering hand; the pretty, brown, beaded slipper that peeped from a cloud of white lace skirts, the little pink ear embedded in her golden, wind-tossed tresses. As he was passing she glanced up at him. For one instant he looked full into her face, and felt that the burning admiration of his eyes had claimed her notice, for she looked down with faintly heightened color.

Never before had Morton felt as he did at that moment. His blood ran in hot streams through his veins. The portals of a new and fascinating experience had opened to him. He walked round to the other side of the hotel, trying in vain to drive the girl and her eyes from his mind. He laughed at himself, and struggled a little against the strange sensation which had taken possession of him. " What a pure creature she must be ! " he thought; how different from himself ! He shuddered, and a strange discontent stole over him. He was examining himself under a microscope of self-contempt, as it were, and it revealed his short-comings with startling distinctness. What an angel was the girl he had just passed !

All at once the presence of the moving throng grated upon him. He left the veranda, and strolled down the side of the mountain. Seating himself on a grass-grown bowlder, he began to map out his literary plans for the future. He would write down everything worthy of note ; nothing should escape him. He would study the habits and the dialect of the negroes, and—but what had become of his enthusiasm ? Why did that Southern girl's face and eyes haunt him ? Then he gave up trying to evade his thoughts, and found it delicious, there in the balmy air, to build fancies about her, and to recall her beauty and the exquisite tone of her voice.

In the evening the music of the orchestra drew Morton to the dining-room. The tables had been removed, and the guests, in evening dress, were preparing to dance. Morton's eye swept restlessly over the assembly, seeking the subject of his thoughts; but she was not in sight.

Feeling very lonely, he left the room and walked out upon the now almost deserted balcony. Here and there sat a couple enjoying the cool breeze, which kept the tops of the mountain trees in gentle motion. The strains of the orchestra and the shuffling of feet followed him. In one of the large parlors some one was playing on a piano, and through the open windows he could see a merry cluster of little girls dancing. The katydids were singing in the trees, and a gauzy ocean of shimmering clouds hovered over the valley. In his purer moments of retrospection, Morton had a habit of recalling to mind a little sister of his who had died years before. She was the companion of his loneliness now. She had been ambitious for a child; she used to tell him that some day she would try to make a name for herself. She had always felt that she could

succeed as an actress. She used to recite to
him and was satisfied with her efforts only
when he was pleased. He had been her ideal
of perfect manhood.

His eyes grew moist; a weight was on his
breast. " Poor Lilly ! " he sighed. How he
wished that she had lived ! She would have
been happy indeed over the fame he had
already acquired, for she had been proud of
him when he had accomplished nothing.

" May I trouble you for a match, sir ? "

He was roused from his reverie with a start.
The father of the girl who had so deeply interested him was at his side, holding a cigar between his fingers. Morton gave him a match,
lifting his hat as he did so.

" Thank you," said the old man ; " will you
smoke ? "

Morton accepted the proffered cigar, feeling
a strange delight surge over him as the old
gentleman held out the burning match to him.

" You, like myself, are not dancing to-
night," went on the old man, as he blew a
cloud of smoke from his lips. " I am getting
too old for that now ; besides, my wife is unwell, and never comes down at night. But

you are young; I should think you would enjoy it."

"I am a stranger," said Morton; "I arrived only this morning."

"I see, I see," returned the former, pleasantly. "Well, we—that is my daughter and myself—do not know many of the guests here. Stanton is my name, sir. You will pardon my introducing myself, but we of the old school in the South do not stand much on ceremony. I live down at G——, a small town in Georgia."

So foreign was any idea of deception to Edgar's present mood, that it was on his tongue to give his real name; but he remembered himself suddenly.

"My name is Dudley—Marshal Dudley," he said, with slow awkwardness—"from Boston."

"I am pleased to meet you, sir, and if I can do anything to make your stay here agreeable I shall be glad to do so."

In the conversation which ensued between the two men during the next half-hour, Morton bent his every energy toward pleasing his new acquaintance. And he succeeded to an extent that surprised himself. They talked of politics, religion, literature, art, and the late war, commenting now and then on the scenery. Mr. Stanton's conversation was easy and intellectual; he evinced pleasure in speaking of matters of local historic interest to such a willing listener.

"Really, sir, I am delighted to have formed your acquaintance," he was saying, when his daughter emerged from a hallway and came hastily to him.

"Why, papa, I've been looking for you everywhere!" she ejaculated, with a sweet, undulant intonation, and breathing hard, as if she had been walking rapidly.

She wore a gown cut low enough at the neck to expose her snowy throat and a drift of diaphanous lace about her bosom. Under the blended rays from the moon and the gas overhead she looked like a breathing, tinted statue.

"Papa," she went on, "I am really afraid this night air will make you sick. You ought not to be here without your hat; how imprudent!"

Mr. Stanton turned to her with a beaming face:

"Ah, it's you, daughter! So I have been disobeying orders again; well, I have always been a slave to the caprices of women. But, Irene, I want to introduce you to a new

3

acquaintance of mine—Mr. Dudley, from Boston."

She looked into Morton's eyes frankly, and, with almost hidden hesitation, gave him her soft, warm hand.

" I am pleased to meet you," she said, and turned to her father.

" Papa, I came to tell you that mamma wants you ; she is still sitting up."

A faint shadow fell athwart Mr. Stanton's wrinkled visage.

" Well, all right," he said, pleasantly, as he turned to go; " I will run up to her; you may stay and entertain Mr. Dudley. Remember, he is a total stranger, and do not let the South's reputation for hospitality suffer at your hands."

CHAPTER IV.

MORTON felt as if he were in a delightful dream. He was almost spellbound by her charm of person. For once in his life he felt a little awkward. His eyes betrayed his mute admiration, and her face flushed slightly under his glance.

"It is a sublime view from here," said she, drawing a light shawl round her perfect shoulders, and looking out into the moonlight. "I would be content to live here always."

"You love nature, then?"

"Very much."

"You have a poetic soul; it is natural."

She started at his frank remark, and looked at him in surprise.

"How do you know?"

Her tone was rather disconcerted, but earnest. They were standing side by side on the edge of the balcony. Morton had frequently amused himself with a certain skilful trick of paying deserved compliments to ladies in a most unconventional manner. He smiled, and looked at her steadily.

"You cannot hide it. Pardon me if I seem too free, but an air of poesy seems to pervade your every movement; it flutters like an imprisoned bird in your voice; it beams like the fire of burning fancies in your eyes."

"Oh, how absurd!"

A faint smile came to life on her lips, and quickly died. She seemed about to take umbrage at what he had said. She looked at him steadily, even haughtily, for an instant, but the sincerity in his eyes disarmed her, as he felt it would.

"You are jesting, Mr. Dudley," said she, in a low, quivering voice; and there was a virginal sensitiveness in her helpless face that touched him sharply. "Because—because one confesses to loving such a night-scene as this, ought one to be accused of being poetical, sentimental?"

"No, not sentimental," he smiled. "But you will have to pardon me for my frankness; I have an unfortunate habit of reading people by their faces, and when I arrive at a conclu-

sion I feel a certain right to it. Indeed, I cannot
conscientiously retract what I said in regard
to your poetic nature. Look !" They were walking slowly past a door through which the ball-
room could be seen. " Such a scene to the average woman's eye, is about the most attractive
one on earth. Note how their eyes gleam ;
see how they smile ; listen to their laughter,
their incessant chatter ; watch them as they
move in the dance. Their every vein is throb-
bing with pleasurable emotions. Hardly one
of them would leave it for a moment to enjoy
the sublimity of this view. Pardon me, but I
think you would find your horizon obscured in
such a crowd. You might mingle with them
as a sort of social duty ; but your better self
would not be there ; you love Infinity too
deeply."

She laughed, but not naturally.

"How do you know so much ? " she said,
visibly gratified by what she felt to be truth ;
" you may be quite wrong."

" I don't claim to be infallible," he returned,
in a tone which he knew well how to assume, but in which now, almost to his surprise,
lurked no little true feeling ; " but really,

Miss Stanton, I know that your tastes are far
above the average woman's. I noticed you to-
day with your father, and I have been hoping
ever since that I might meet you."

She gave him a fleeting, timid glance, and
dropped her head. She thought it strange
that he should know her disposition so well.
She had trusted few young men in her life,
but as this handsome stranger regarded her
with his warm, admiring glance, she was beginning to think that she could trust him; and
as they walked to and fro she unconsciously
leaned more confidingly on his arm.

"I thank you; you are very kind," she said,
sweetly. "Papa is very thoughtful of the
comfort of strangers."

On reaching a side door leading into the
ball-room, they paused and looked in. The
orchestra was playing a delightful waltz; the
floor was invitingly smooth.

"I do not dance very well," said Morton,
"but I should like very much to waltz with
you."

She bowed her head, and preceded him
into the ball-room. Under the bright light
her attire was most becoming. She wore a

pale-blue muslin, with white roses on her shoulders and at her belt. Morton felt her beauty and supple grace take possession of his senses like the spell of some strange enchantment. He was all aglow as he placed his arm around her shapely waist. From her luxuriant hair an odor of fresh violets was wafted, her eyes were indescribable; through her thin glove the hand he held felt delightfully soft, and magnetic. She danced perfectly; their steps accorded well.

"You dance better than any one I know," he said, in her ear, while they were gliding through the whirling crowd.

She murmured her appreciation of the compliment. Her warm breath touched his cheek, and he took a firmer clasp upon her hand.

After the waltz, he drew his companion back on to the veranda. He was afraid that some one else would ask her to dance. And his fears were well-grounded, for just as they were taking seats in an almost deserted part of the balcony, two young men hastened up.

"Oh, Miss Stanton," exclaimed the one who reached her first, "will you not dance the next waltz with me?"

"I am very sorry, Mr. Jones," she said, "but I do not wish to dance any more to-night, I shall have to go up to my mother pretty soon, and I am tired now."

"I came to ask the same favor, Miss Stanton," said the other young man, "but Mr. Jones's defeat means my downfall."

After the young men had left, both Morton and his companion were silent for a few moments. The music and hum from the ball-room scarce reached their ears ; the shrill tones of the clarionet, rising independent of the other instruments, seemed the weird cry of some wind-tossed mountain bird. Four negroes, waiters in the dining-room, passed. One of them was thrumming on a guitar strapped across his breast. They stopped near by, and began to sing a quaint plantation song to the guitar's responsive accompaniment. The singers were to music born ; their voices blended together in perfect harmony.

"You can easily imagine how I enjoy their singing, Miss Stanton," said Morton ; "I have heard few colored people sing in my life."

"I suppose you do," she replied. "I have heard such melodies all my life, but I never

tire of them. They make up their songs;
there is little rhythm to the words; listen!"

Morton smiled as he paid close attention to
the next stanza:

> "No time fer ter eat, no time fer ter drink,
>   Git erlong, oh! git erlong!
> Devil ketch yer 'fo' yer kin wink,
>   Git erlong, oh! git erlong!"

After singing several songs, the vocalists
bow themselves away, hat in hand. From the
subject of music the conversation turned upon
literature, and Morton experienced an unpleasant sensation as she began to speak of
American authors. He felt that he could meet
any emergency rather than have her even inci-
dentally allude to his efforts. He purposely
changed the subject.

"Pardon my being personal again," said he,
believing that what he was about to say would
please her, so thoroughly had he read her
nature, "but I feel sure that you write; that
you aspire to; at least——" he hesitated, floun-
dering in the mire of a very delicate situation, for
her eyes were fixed steadily, almost resentfully,
upon him. "Your criticisms have been so

clear, so unique," he went on. "Indeed, I have always found the best critics the most competent judges of what is best in literature among literary workers."

She dropped her lashes. The warm blood rose and struggled in her delicious face. She did not speak for a moment, then she said, sighing lightly :

"I believe you are a wizard. There is no use in my trying to hide anything from you; you know me already as well as my father does. I should have been offended if any other stranger had been so candid with me, but it seems as if I had known you a long time. You are right about my aspirations; since childhood I have felt an unconquerable desire to become an authoress. I have never written for publication, but have composed and destroyed hundreds of things. There are times when I feel that I simply have to write. I have never talked so freely with a young man before. You are not like those I know; you seem to think and to feel as I do about most things. My society friends laugh at my ideas, and make me disgusted with myself, but you seem to understand me."

Morton almost feared that his face would betray the inward satisfaction he felt over the compliment she had paid him. He saw himself on the direct road to her esteem. She liked him because his tastes agreed with hers ; she should have no cause to feel otherwise.

"I have had my dreams, too," he said, with almost natural pensiveness, so thoroughly was his heart in the *rôle* he was enacting. "I have dreamed of many victories, but my dreams have resulted in nothing so far."

She was silent, seemingly lost in reflection, her great, pensive eyes looking down the mountain's side where, among the trees, lay an army of weather-stained bowlders. The promenaders were at the other end of the veranda ; the music from the ball-room sounded soft and low, mingled with the slurring of tripping feet. The dusky serenaders had gone down the rocky slope to a cottage, and their melodious voices were wafted back on the breeze. As low and subdued as if the bell were buried in the heart of the mountain came the strokes of a clock in Chattanooga. She counted them, noting each metallic, wind-borne sigh by touching the balustrade with her white hand.

" Ten ! " she exclaimed, in a tone of mingled
surprise and regret, " I had no idea it was
so late. I have not remained downstairs so
long since mamma's illness."

She rose rather hurriedly, and gave him her
hand.

" Good-night," she said, and turned away.

" Good-night," he echoed with regret in his
voice, and he watched her till she entered the
hall near by.

He was in no humor to mingle with others,
so he went up to his room. On a table lay his
tin-encased typewriter, which he carried with
him wherever he went. It reminded him un-
pleasantly of his working-room in New York.
It occurred to him to uncover the machine to
see if any of its parts had been injured by trans-
portation, but he was not in the humor then.
He felt very feverish and sat down in an open
window. The night view invited thought,
and he fell into serious and discontented reflection.

His better nature had been sounded to deeps
which the plummet of conscience had not
touched for years. He examined his callous
nature as if it were some loathsome thing be-

neath a microscope.   After all his plans, his
aspirations, what was he?   What right had he
to fame?   He thought of Jean Wharton, and
became more miserable than ever.   He threw
his cigar, just lighted, out of the window and
watched its sparks shower through the boughs
of a young oak as it fell to earth.   His thoughts
kept him awake till late in the night.   Irene
was in his mind's eye, her voice in his ear.
How happy she would make some man—some
worthy man!   He tried to think of his plans,
but she filled every nook and cranny of his
brain.   At last he dropped to sleep and in his
dreams he was continually groping after some
vague, phantom happiness.

CHAPTER V.

MORTON's slumbers were broken with the first appearance of day in the eastern skies. So filled had his dreams been with struggling fancies that he felt languid from lack of rest. Finding that he could not go to sleep again, he rose and dressed himself.

From his window he saw the great golden orb of day rise from a diaphanous sea of clouds in the valley, and climb towards the spotless zenith. He went below; few guests were up. There was something soothing in the quiet which hovered over the general disorder, like the ghost of departed mirth. The servants were replacing the chairs and tables in the dining-room and sweeping off the verandas. The night clerk in the office was giving place to his freshly-washed, damp-haired successor for the day and whistling a sleepy air as he ran over a memorandum.

The parlors had a slovenly aspect. A handkerchief-crowned black girl was brushing the furniture, arranging dishevelled music sheets, and picking up playing-cards, books, and fans, which were strewn in wild disorder over tables and carpets.

Edgar went to the spot where he had last sat with Irene. He found the two chairs just as he and Irene had left them. Under the one which she had used lay a dainty cambric handkerchief. He felt his heart throb as he picked it up, damp with dew, and scented with the odor of violets. As he spread the delicate thing upon his knee, a tender, reverential feeling stole over him. Then he put it carefully away in his breast-pocket, and began to picture to himself how its owner had looked as she sat in the chair by him in the moonlight.

He remained there till the guests began to emerge from their rooms and walk about the ground. An old married couple, with heads erect and nostrils distended, were drinking in the fresh air as they strolled down the road into the sun-mellowed haze, which deepened into a fog beneath the trees. On the balcony above, a nurse was rolling an infant in a perambulator, the wheels of which rumbled like

distant thunder. A wealthy *blasé* young
devotee to society was enduring the unctuous
flattery of the mother of a beautiful but moneyless daughter, as he half sat, half reclined in a
hammock, smoking a cigar. Some one began
to play on a piano somewhere upstairs; and a
little girl passed, tossing up an apple and catching it in her hands. The click, click of billiard
balls was heard, mingled with the clatter and
crash of dishes from the kitchen and the roar
and thump of a ten-pin alley. Some one threw
a champagne bottle from a window upstairs,
and it gurgled and whistled and shrieked till
it crashed upon a rock down the slope.

Mrs. Stanton being worse than usual, her
daughter remained with her all day, and it was
not till the following morning that Morton
was rewarded by a sight of Irene. He saw her
pass along the veranda and walk down the
steps toward the wood below the hotel. He
felt his face grow cold, and his heart almost
ceased to beat. She had not seen him. He
hesitated a moment as to whether he might
follow her. Before he could make up his mind
to do so she had vanished behind the long
building.

He descended the veranda steps hesitatingly ; but when he had turned the corner she was not in sight, and the wood and two diverging paths confronted him.　One led up to the mountain-top, the other down the sheer incline.　He hastened along the first, hoping to catch sight of her, but was disappointed.

He turned back, vexed with himself.　He knew then that she had gone down among the great rocks to the picturesque cliffs, and when he had returned to the divergence of the paths, the temptation to seek her by the un-tried way was too strong to be resisted.　Pres-ently, following the steep, rugged path, he saw her.　She was sitting upon the extreme edge of the highest cliff on the mountain, her figure clearly outlined against the blue sky.

She was not aware of his approach even when he paused among the stunted bushes quite near her.　She was bewitchingly pretty in her re-pose of face and form.　She wore a well-fitting, tailor-made gown of gray, and a broad-brimmed, black straw hat, beneath which her wavy tresses lay like molten gold.　In her lap she held a portfolio, and was sketching the landscape. Rapidly and gracefully her hand moved over

4

the wind-fluttered paper. Edgar was wondering
how he could best make his presence known,
when his foot dislodged a stone, which rolled
down toward her. She looked up at him with
a start; a transient quiver of recognition disturbed her features: she colored a little, and then
a slow smile dawned in her eyes and spread over
her face.

"Pardon my boldness," said he, respectfully
removing his hat and descending to her. "I
saw you pass the veranda and could not resist
the temptation to follow you."

"You are quite welcome," she returned,
simply, closing her portfolio, and endeavoring
to hide it at her side.

Despite his foibles, Morton had a good deal
of the knightly element in his composition.
He certainly looked a model of courtly grace
and exceptionally handsome as he stood, hat
in hand, the rays of the sun playing on his
shining hair.

"The view is sublime from here," he said,
introductively.

"Yes," she acquiesced; "I have been coming to this spot almost every day since we
arrived. I almost worship it."

She took note of the seeming delicacy of feeling which kept him from seating himself near her, and regarded his uncovered head as a mute offering of respect.

"You were sketching," said he, catching the branch of a bush between his fingers with a nervousness that was novel to him.

"It could hardly be termed that," said she, with heightened color; "but I love this spot so much that I wanted to take something home with me, even if it was only a very little like it."

"I should be delighted to see your work, if you do not mind," he ventured. "You would find me very sympathetic."

There was a struggle between inclination and hesitation in her face; her hands trembled as she turned over the sheets, but she took out the sketch and handed it to him.

"Please do not think I consider it good," she said, almost imploringly. "I have never had a teacher."

He scrutinized the sketch closely, uncertain which he admired most at the moment, her fluttering timidity in regard to her work, or the work itself. Her watchful eyes discerned genuine appreciation in his face.

"Undeniably, you have talent," said he, slowly, seating himself on a stone near her. He spoke with such evident sincerity that she offered no protest. "You have never had a teacher?" he went on, looking at her face, and feeling that his eyes ratified his praise. "Your work is wonderful."

She was too true and unconventional even to assume a look of doubt as to his earnestness; besides, she had always believed she had undeveloped power. She met his look with eyes from which her very soul seemed bubbling into lambent light.

"No, I have not been so fortunate," she said, almost breathlessly.

"I can see that," said he, feeling that his implied criticism would only strengthen her confidence in him and her appreciation of his praise. He looked from the picture to the grand view of valleys, hills, and undulating land that stretched away in the hazy air toward the west. "But you have genius, your pencil is one of those that need little guidance."

As he took her pencil and pointed out a few places where her work might be improved, she leaned toward him. Her face was near his shoulder; he could almost feel its warmth. Her pretty hands were clasped over her knees, in wondering, childlike eagerness.

"Oh, I see, I see!" she exclaimed. "Thank you; I'm so glad you showed me; I never could see that before. I have tried so hard to make the trees down there look as if the wind were really blowing through their leaves!"

As he artfully ran a pencil over the foliage of one of her trees she watched him with a glance of mingled gratitude and admiration. She took the sheet and looked at it for a moment, then put it into her portfolio, her face losing a portion of its impulsive warmth.

"I did not know that you could sketch," she said, almost coldly.

"Nor can I," he said, quickly, seeing her drift; "I only learned that little trick from an artist friend whom I used to know. I could not do the work you have done to save my life."

Her susceptible visage showed the sudden departure of the doubt she had half entertained.

"I want to thank you," he pursued, "for the delightful evening you gave me. I missed you sadly all day yesterday."

"Mamma was ill," she said, in a sweet, pathetic

tremolo. And she dropped her glance down among the frightful crags and fissures below. " She fell on the stairs a month ago and struck her head. There is a sort of depression upon the brain, the doctors say. At times she is out of her right mind. The physicians advised us to bring her here ; they thought the change would benefit her ; but she is no better, and so we are going home to-morrow."

" Home? To-morrow ? " his tone was so earnest and regretful that she looked at him wonderingly.

" Yes ; we must go in the morning ; mamma desires it very much."

She seemed to appreciate the interest with which he listened to her as she went on and spoke with charming frankness of her home affairs.

" We are very poor," she said, with a faint, apologetic smile. " We own our home, however, and some of our old slaves are still with us ; but we have a hard time making ends meet. Our house is much larger than we need, so some of the young business men of the town board with us. They are not the slightest trouble, and will submit to any sort of house-

keeping.   My aunt is seeing to things in our
absence.   Old Millie, our cook, is perfection ;
and Aunt Del is a most excellent servant.   Besides, there are Uncle Tony and half-a-dozen
little darkies of all sizes.   But really I must be
going ; the morning has passed rapidly."

The stone upon which she sat rested on a
great rock, which sloped off sharply to the edge
of the cliff.   As she rose she stepped upon a
pencil that had dropped from her lap ; it
turned beneath her foot, and before he could
render assistance, she had fallen and three
fourths of her body had disappeared over the
precipice.   By the merest chance her feet
caught upon some projecting part of the cliff's
face, and with her hands pressed tightly against
the top, she held herself poised, her head and
shoulders only in view.

He sprang toward her ; but as he bent down
over her he saw that he would be powerless to
lift her, for he could not possibly brace his feet
firmly enough upon the sloping stone.   He did
not even dare to release her hands from the rock,
knowing that he could not support her weight.
She had not uttered a cry, but when she saw
him bending over her, she cried out firmly :

" No, you cannot hold me; your feet will slip ;
it's too steep ! "

Her poor, tortured face was as pale as ashes.
He knew she was right, and his heart stood
still—his head swam at the frightful depth.
It was hundreds of feet to the jagged stones
beneath ; the tall trees in the valley seemed
mere shrubs, over which the clouds had hung
a semi-transparent veil.

" Oh, I am falling ! It's giving way ! " she
screamed, in terror.

He heard the crunching of crumbling stone,
and saw her begin to sink. As quick as lightning
it occurred to him that with his body prone upon
the rock he might hold her; so he threw himself down on his side and grasped her arms
just as her support gave way and went rattling
down below. Her weight fell suddenly upon
his arms, drawing him down perilously near the
brink.

To lessen the strain on his arms he drew her
firmly against the rock. He felt that it would be
impossible for him to lift her into safety, owing
to the frailty of his hold. It was the crucial
test of Morton's moral manhood. All his life
he had had a superstitious dread of death, and

had sincerely doubted that he could ever, under any circumstances, have the courage to sacrifice his own life to save another's. He knew that to release her would guarantee his safety, and believed that to cling to her a moment longer meant sure death to both ; and yet he held on, feeling his soul swell with an exaltation he had never felt before. He felt the strength of ten men in his arms. She comprehended the situation, and said, very calmly :

"Release me, and save yourself ; you cannot aid me ; you will lose your own life ; let me go."

"No ! no ! " he cried out, in sudden horror, as she moved slightly from him.

She was wordless and still, but gave him a glance from her big, soulful eyes that renewed his strength. He felt that if he could only depend on his hold upon the rock he might draw her up to him, but there was scarcely a chance in his favor. He listened for a moment, hoping to hear the sound of approaching help, but everything was as quiet as the grave.

"Be perfectly still ! " he cautioned, firmly. "If you stir we shall both be lost ; I shall never let you go."

She closed her eyes to keep from seeing the

purple agony of his face as he began to draw
her closer to him. In his almost superhuman
effort he pressed his shoulder so firmly against
the rock that his legs were drawn down till
they lay parallel with the sharp verge of the
precipice. His hold was true. He succeeded
in drawing her breast over upon his as he
slowly turned upon his back. Then, holding
her to him with his left arm, he cautiously
clutched the skirt of her gown with his right
hand and gradually drew her upon him. But
just as her whole limp form settled in its
full length upon his, they slowly slid, powerless
to stop themselves, down till the very edge of
the cliff touched the middle of his back, and
there they miraculously paused.

"For God's sake, don't stir!" he whispered
under his breath.

Her face almost touched his; her hair fell in
a shimmering mass round his neck. It seemed
to him that he held himself in that frightful
poise only through sheer tension of his muscles
and by dominating his body to his will. She
was holding her breath, and had fully comprehended their peril. Her eyes were on his; she
was in his tight embrace. A moment, which

seemed an hour, passed. Then, in the very
yawning mouth of eternity, her sensitive, virginal nature began to cast blood-filtered shadows
upon her face. She tried to avoid his eyes,
and yet feared to move so much as an eyelid.
He witnessed her mental struggle, and a warm
thrill of poetic admiration went through his
frame. Then he saw her visage begin to raise
the ashy flag of defeat; her eyes were drooping, her lips drawn. She was fainting, not
through fear of death, but on account of a
situation more horrible to her mind.

"For God's sake, do not faint!" he pleaded
without a motion of his breast." We are lost if
you do. I could not hold your dead weight!"

She rallied; her face hardened under its robe
of white. He read her determination that he
should not lose his life through weakness of
hers.

"It would be useless to remain longer as
we are," he said, with a look in his eyes that
she understood. "Can't you get a little hold
upon an unevenness in the rocks?"

She glanced aside very cautiously, and then
said, under her breath:

"There is a little place, but I am afraid to

risk it. I could not reach it and hold you; you would fall."

"Do not mind me," he said; "save yourself."

She did not look in the direction of the place again, but gazed into his eyes an instant and then closed her own. He saw that she was praying. He felt himself growing weaker. In a few seconds all would be over. Edgar Morton had never faced death before, but he met it now without a fear. His sole aim was to save the woman in his arms. He thought of throwing her on the rock above him, but instantly saw that even that was impracticable, for he had not sufficient strength left. Then the hope flashed through his brain that he might get a slight hold upon the face of the cliff beneath him if he could safely lower his hand. He reflected an instant, then whispered to her to lean slowly toward the mountain as he put out his arm in the opposite direction. She obeyed so gradually, and his hand moved so cautiously, that his body did not stir. Then he felt the rough cliff's face under his fingers, and his heart bounded as his thumb went into a small, firm fissure.

"Thank God!" he panted, "I can hold now; but get up cautiously."

She crawled slowly from him, but held on to his clothing as anxiously as if she were acting for her soul, and he were her physical self. The mute action filled him with a strange languorous delight. Slowly he wormed himself, aided by her hands, back upon the rock, and crawled after her up to the little plateau above. He sat up and laughed, without making a sound; his face was almost luminously pale; the mountain seemed to him to be bowing to the sun. She saw that he was fainting, and caught him in her arms. As consciousness left him he knew only that his head was in her lap, that her hands were on his face. Their icy touch revived him. He looked like a dead person in whose eyes the glimmer of a soul still lingers. Then he remembered himself, and sat up. Both were speechless; she held his hand, rubbing it mutely, almost hysterically.

"We had a narrow escape," said he, finding voice at last, and smiling to mask his weakness.

"You saved my life——"

She broke down, and raised her hands to her white face. They were bleeding from several scratches. He had a sudden desire to press them to his lips and kiss away the blood, but had she been a queen, and he her vilest subject, he could not have felt less worthy.

"You saved mine," he panted. "If you had moved when I asked you not to I should have been lost. I understood your sacrifice, and I want you to know that I did."

Her face waxed red in spots; a sort of tear-haze came into her eyes. She rose slowly and looked down at him. Had she mutely held out her arms she could not have shown him better what he had become to her. He got up and stood swaying beside her, as languorously blissful as if he were dreaming of dying before the open gates of heaven.

"I can never express a thousandth part of my gratitude," she murmured, slowly turning toward the homeward path.

"We will say no more about it," he said. "I did nothing; I could not have seen you fall down there if I had tried. Really it was not I who did it; it was something in me better than I have ever been."

She did not reply. He gallantly extended his faltering hand to assist her up the path, which was very steep for a few yards ; but she refused it, and without a word of explanation, caught his arm and with almost masculine strength helped him up the incline.

They had almost reached the hotel, when he suddenly stopped, as if confronted by an unpleasant thought, and stared into her eyes.

" You go away in the morning ? "

" Yes."

His breast was wrung with pain, for a moment, then an inward fire illumined his face.

"I could go to G——," he said; "why not? I came to see the country, and—and if your father takes boarders, I might even go to your house. I should like it very much—that is, if you do not mind."

All the mingled tenderness, joy and gratitude of which her nature was capable seemed to ignite and burn in her eyes and face. She tried to express her gladness, but her voice was still as air in the bubble of a crystal. She simply put out her quivering hand till it touched his. He understood, and went on, with the happy enthusiasm of a schoolboy:

"Well, I shall follow you day after tomorrow, if—if——"

She looked up suddenly, almost fearfully.

"If I can wait that long."

He parted from her at a side door of the hotel, and went up to his room to lie down to rest and to—think.

CHAPTER VI.

THE home of the Stantons, in the suburbs of a small southern town, was a grand old place. The air of antiquity pervading it captured Morton's fancy.

It was a square, two-storied brick building with a long white veranda in front and a shorter one on the back, connected by a wide hall through the building. It stood some distance from the street, upon an extensive lawn, shaded by numerous oaks, china trees, magnolias and cedars, and interspersed with poorly-kept parterres filled with flowers and weeds. Here and there, embrowned and gnawed by time, was a dank, vine-covered summer-house, whose moss-laden roof threatened to crush its frail trellised walls to earth. At the side of the house stood three or four old frame cottages occupied by negroes.

There was a home like look about the place that inspired Morton with a new sense of restful-

5

ness. His young career had been such an active
one, and yet so solitary, that the prospect of stay-
ing a while in such retirement, and of growing
more intimate with such people as the Stantons,
was most inviting.

Mr. Stanton drove to the station, and took
him home in his old-fashioned buggy. In
response to a delicate query, Morton was informed that Mrs. Stanton was much better,
though still confined to her room.

As they neared the house, Edgar's heart
bounded at the sight of Irene's trim figure
among the vines on the veranda. He was one
of those students of human emotions by whom
few expressive faces pass unread, whose ears
interpret almost every tone of voice. As he
drew near, her eyes fell for an instant and a
bright glow came into her face, then she looked
up and came toward him, smiling. In her
softened bearing and timidity, as she gave him
her hand and spoke a few simple words of welcome, there was an indescribable something that
sank into his heart.

She excused herself and withdrew when a
servant came to direct him upstairs to the room
allotted to his use. Descending later he found

Mr. Stanton on the veranda, talking to Mrs. Livingston, his widowed sister. Edgar was introduced to her and to the three young men boarders as they came in from their work for the evening meal. The tea-bell rang, and as they were all walking out to the dining-room, Irene joined him in the wide, lamp-lighted hall.

"I was not sure you would come so soon," she said, as they fell back a little behind the others, "and now that you are here I am afraid you will be somewhat disappointed with this quiet place after leaving such a gay resort as Lookout Mountain."

"Oh, but this old town is very interesting," he replied. "I find so much to charm one; I am really tempted not to extend my journey further South."

"Papa, did you hear that?" she asked her parent across the table, after Morton, obeying Mrs. Livingston's invitation, had taken a seat beside Irene. "Mr. Dudley is already so favorably impressed with G—— that he is tempted to go no further South. Indeed, you must have been quite entertaining in your drive from the depot."

Morton winced at the sound of his assumed

name. He decided that he would take the first opportunity to confess his disguise to her and her father; he had not been satisfied with his *rôle* since his talk with Irene on the cliff.

"I am glad," Mr. Stanton returned. "I can well understand the charm that such a place would have for a Bostonian."

Then Mr. Brown, a raw-boned, side-whiskered young man with eyes of a sort of blue, like the color of whey, and who was a clerk in a dry-goods store, ventured to remark, looking across at the new-comer with interest,

"You are from Boston, sir? I'm Southern 'to the backbone,' as the expression goes, and I acknowledge I ain't too fond of the North and her people, considering what she has brought us to; but I have met some very nice men from Boston. Boston is a sort of an oasis in the desert of that country, anyway, so I have heard."

Everybody laughed at Mr. Brown's wit except Irene. Morton fancied he saw a shadow of disapproval flit across her face.

"Mr. Brown is the manager of our Young Men's Christian Association," she explained, sweetly.

"We would be glad to have you come round to our quarters, Mr. Dudley," put in Brown, cordially. "We have a little reading-room, and a number of papers on file. You must consider yourself welcome at any time. Are you a member of the Association in Boston?"

Morton regretted to say that he had never joined; that he had always had so many other duties to perform; that,—indeed, it was not exactly in his way.

Brown's milk-and-curd eyes rolled ominously. He looked at the two young men at his side as if to inquire if they had heard the remarkable confession, and then stared fixedly at his plate. He had nothing more to say, and he felt that his silence and his whiskers were very impressive.

"Oh, Mr. Brown is so funny!" laughed Irene, as she and Morton walked into the spacious, old-time parlor, after the young men had gone back to business. "You will overlook all his peculiarities when you know him; he is such an interesting, comical study. There was never another like him."

Morton was charmed with the room. The

fireplace was wide, high, and deep, the mantel
heavy and old-styled. There was an old-fashioned piano with age-yellowed keys and sloping,
octagonal legs. Against a wall stood a tall book-
case, at each side of which hung some weather-
cracked portraits of men and women of the
ancien régime. A round table in the centre
of the room was noticeable for its massive
antiquity; the lace curtains which hung from
gilt cornices were very heavy and dingy with
age.

It being warm indoors, Irene led him through
an open window on to the front veranda, where
stood some chairs and rustic benches. From
one of the tall, white columns, to a ring in the
facing of a window, a hammock was suspended.
She gracefully seated herself in it, her hands
stretching out to its ropes, and her pretty feet
just tipping the floor. The gloaming was
brightening into poetic moonlight; the crickets
in the grass and trees were shrilling. A church
bell, swinging in a wooden tower near a little
brick church, beyond a patch of tasselled corn,
was ringing for prayer-meeting. In the heart
of the town an amateur cornetist was sputtering
out a doleful air; a deep-voiced negro was sing-

ing behind the kitchen; some one in the woods
in the rear of the house was calling hogs in
mellow, bovine tones: "Pigoop, pigoo! pigoop,
pigoo!" and the dull whack of a wood-cutter's
axe fell into the general dissonance. Flowers
in crude boxes, broken fruit-jars, and cracked
basins stood on the window-sills; and the perfume of fuschias, geraniums, and clematis filled
the air. Myriads of flashing lightning-bugs
bespangled the deeper darkness beneath the
trees and arbors.

Morton seated himself in a chair near the
hammock. Since entering upon his literary
career he had enjoyed hardly a moment's rest
from thinking over his work; but he recked
little of it now. There was no room in his
heart or brain for anything aside from the girl
before him.

Both were silent for a few moments. He put
out his hand to the hammock and began to pro-
pel it gently to and fro, experiencing a delicate,
thrilling sense of enjoyment whenever he drew
her toward him.

Her voice first broke the silence.

"I have been wondering what profession you
belong to, Mr. Dudley," she said, timidly. "I

know I have no right to ask, but you are so
artistic in your tastes, so unlike ordinary men,
that——"

She paused. He felt that he ought to confess all to her; and yet it seemed so difficult,
while her pure eyes were looking so confidingly
into his, to acknowledge the part he had played.
He evaded the question; he could not answer
then, but he resolved to do so very soon.

" I am really nothing worth speaking of," he
said; " you compliment me most highly. Of
course, I can't deny that I am ambitious. I
have known and sympathized with many suc-
cessful literary people ; some of them have even
told me that I encouraged them. It has given
me no little pleasure to hope that I may, perhaps, be able to advise you. You have too
much talent to allow it to go uncared for."

She looked at him with steady eyes. She put
her foot firmly on the floor, and the hammock
came to a standstill.

" What do you think I ought to do ? " she
asked, softly.

Her face was not far from his. The wither-
ing roses at her white neck trembled so that
some of their leaves fell into her lap. He had

never seen such a perfect, poetic face; the suppressed power of her intellectual longings stamped it with the highest imprint of human beauty.

" You ought to write," said he, with secret pride in the sincerity of his words. " On the evening I first met you, you told me that you had been doing so for years for your own amusement. It has been my fortune," he continued, carefully weighing his words lest he should betray himself, " to associate intimately with editors and publishers. I was once employed as a reader of manuscripts for a leading magazine and publishing house. I don't know why they valued my opinion, but I confess they did. In that position I read the first productions of many new writers, some of whom are now famous. I have already seen so much in you that I should like to examine your work. I should like to aid you—at least to encourage you to persevere."

Had he cudgelled his brain for months he could have said nothing which would have raised him higher in her estimation. The poor girl had felt such longings to be heard by the world that she reverenced the very thread

which held a magazine or a book together. As
a child she had written little stories on tiny
sheets of paper, which she had bound into
books and prized more than any of her playthings. She had felt a strange sort of awe
when in the presence of the only editor in the
town, and she used to spell out the long words
in his paper, and wonder if he had written all
the stories and poems, which had really been
copied, and why everybody did not respect him
more than the ministers, the doctors, and the
lawyers. Morton's confession, however, threw
a damper on her spirits. For the first time
since she had met him she felt uncomfortable in
his presence. What would he, who had criti-
cized the work of professional writers, think of
her frankness in regard to her own aspirations?
He had doubtless met and turned away hundreds who were perhaps just as hopeful and
deserving as herself. It was true he had spoken
encouragingly to her, but that was because he
knew her, and wished to make himself agreeable. For an instant she was almost angry.
She pushed her feet against the floor, and the
hammock swung back a few inches, causing his
hand to release its hold. Her face colored,

but he did not notice it in the semi-darkness.

"Why are you so silent?" he asked, wondering why she did not reply, and why she was looking at him so steadily.

"I am sorry you did not tell me," she faltered; and he heard her catch her breath. "I ought to have known that you were like that. I should not have talked so much about myself. I hope you will not think——"

She broke down, her bosom rising and falling excitedly. He felt a sympathy for her that he had never experienced before. He put out his hand to the hammock, and drew her nearer to him. He was prevented from replying by the sudden appearance of a servant, who informed Irene that her mother wished to see her. She rose quickly, so quickly indeed that the hammock swung from her before she had firmly placed her feet, and she fell into his arms, which he threw out to catch her. For one instant she rested against his breast, and it required all his strength of will to keep from folding his arms about her. She drew herself from him, blushing deeply.

"I am so awkward," she stammered. "Please forgive me."

He tried to detain her for a moment, but in vain.

He walked with her to the door, and saw her disappear in the darkness of the long hall, leaving him to the dreary companionship of the chairs, the hammock, and the empty moonlight.

CHAPTER VII.

IRENE slowly ascended the stairs. She was very thoughtful. Her heart was heavy. She paused on the stairs for a moment to get composed before going into her mother's presence.

There, in the dark, with one hand pressed on her heart, the other against the wall, she told herself that she had been very foolish. He had been in her thoughts almost constantly since he had acted so nobly on the cliff. She had even fancied she had read a deep regard for her in his eyes, in his tone, that day after the accident; but she now saw her error. He would have done the same for any other girl— for was he not the very embodiment of perfect manhood? His manner and tone had been due to excitement after that terrible ordeal. He had decided to visit G—— in his travels, and she, poor simpleton! had fancied

that she had been instrumental in drawing
him thither.

Mrs. Stanton was sitting at a table, reading,
when her daughter entered. She turned her
gray head, and looked at the flushed face
anxiously.

"Mamma dear, how do you feel now?"
Irene asked, bending over the back of the invalid's chair, and brushing the white, rippling
tresses away from the wrinkled brow.

"I feel better, darling," was the low reply;
"my head has not troubled me all day. I
ought not to have sent for you. I had mis-
laid my glasses and thought you had put them
away, but I found them just now."

"But, mamma, you must not read so much;
you know the doctor has forbidden it."

The mother laid the open book on her knee,
and stroked her daughter's hand caressingly.

"What should I do without you, my pet?"
she asked, tenderly. "You are worth more to
me than all the doctors in the world. But I
shall not read any more to-night." She closed
the book and laid it upon the table. "Now,
my dear, tell me about Mr. Dudley; do you
like him as well as ever?"

Irene was silent. Her mother looked up into her eyes. The girl colored slightly and put her warm cheek against her mother's as she kissed her.

"Well?" said Mrs. Stanton, suddenly thoughtful.

"Yes, mamma; but Mr. Dudley is——"

She was interrupted by her father's entrance.

"Is what, Irene?" he asked, pinching her cheek as he passed over to his easy-chair near his wife. "Out with it, pet; have you found any objection to my paragon of manhood and intellect? Is he an adventurer?"

"No," she laughed, blushing more deeply; "but he is a critic——"

"I knew he was a critic," broke in Mr. Stanton, gravely. "I have yet to meet a man better posted on current events, ethics, politics, art, literature—everything! By Joe! he put me at my wits' end to keep up with his new isms and ologies!"

"No, papa, I don't mean exactly that," plunged Irene beneath the warm waves of confusion; "but he has been literary adviser and critic for one of the leading magazines."

Mr. Stanton refused to be astonished, although his reply came after a significant delay.

"There is really nothing to be wondered at in that, my dear," he said, running his hand through his hair, "for, as I told you, his opinion is valuable. I have thought so ever since he agreed with me on the respective merits of Balzac, Browning, and Hugo. He told me that my criticisms were remarkably strong and to the point."

"I know that, papa," she said, going to him and seating herself on his knee.

He put his arm around her, and his cigar smoke enclouded her head.

"But now is the time for you to improve your opportunities," said he, drawing her fondly against his breast. "The stories which you have been writing and hiding away for the last ten years must be brought out and shown to him. He may be able to do wonders for you. Your sketches of the negroes and our country folk are remarkably strong and well-drawn. He must give us his opinion."

"I would die before he should," said she, very white and firm. "He came here as a boarder, like the others; what right have I to tax his time and patience with my silly writings. Such men are burthened with hundreds of requests. On the mountain I saw the hotel clerk hand him about fifty letters and papers all in a bundle. I know he did not have the time or patience to read them all, for he was smoking on the veranda ten minutes later."

"Well, well, never mind," said the old man, with a strange look in his eyes. "But where did you leave him, my dear?"

"On the front veranda."

"Alone?"

"Yes."

"And here am I, smoking by myself, when I have a whole box of these good cigars just in. I shall go down and offer him one, anyway."

He found Morton gazing out into the mystic moonlight, seated near the hammock.

"Take a cigar," said Mr. Stanton, cheerily.

Morton accepted it, with thanks.

"I am glad to find you alone, Mr. Dudley," began Mr. Stanton, plunging into the subject that was uppermost in his thoughts. "I want to converse with you on a matter that has long interested me deeply. It is in regard to my daughter's talent for writing. I know that

6

you are a competent judge of such matters, and can advise me. I have long entertained strong hopes for her future. She has never been willing to submit her work to the critics. Even I, am obliged, now and then, to steal into her desk to read her writings. I should very much like you to read something by her."

"I should be charmed, delighted!" said Morton, feeling a thrill of anticipation run through him.

"Well, come with me," returned the old man. "Now is a good time, while she is with her mother. I really feel like a thief, but I know I am acting for her good."

He led Morton into a small room at the end of the hall, lighted by a large window, over which an awning of honeysuckle vines hung in rank abundance. There was a vague *cachet* of individuality about everything in it. Some small landscape-paintings in oil hung upon the faded-blue walls. A table in a corner held a collection of books and magazines. Morton's heart rose into his mouth as he noted his "Transgression" among some other modern novels. He would have given anything to possess Irene's candid opinion of his book, and yet he felt an indefinable dread of what that opinion might be. Near the window was a little desk, hardly larger than those used in school-rooms. As Mr. Stanton raised its lid, an old-fashioned inkstand rolled to one side with a rattle and a whir, and Morton felt as if some sacred sacristy were being rudely disturbed. This feeling increased as Mr. Stanton began to fumble about among the neat bundles of snowy manuscript. Morton had never felt so much reverence for anything inanimate before. He put himself in the place of the absent author, remembering that he could never bear to think of any one reading some of his unpublished work.

" Here," said the father, taking out a neatly-folded packet and glancing at the title over his eyeglasses, " here is a short story she wrote last year, a simple tale founded on the death of her old 'mammy.' I have read it several times, but never without tears, for it is very true to nature and strongly pathetic. Pardon me for praising my child's work, but really no one without deep feeling could have produced this."

Morton took the faultlessly-written sheets in his hands. He was so thoughtful, so *distrait*, that Mr. Stanton looked at him wonderingly.

" Will you take something else ? " he questioned, motioning toward the open desk. " She has a good many laid away here."

"Thank you, this will do," said the other, turning away ; " I shall be careful not to soil it. I have never seen a manuscript in more perfect order. I assure you I shall read it with great interest."

Alone in his great, breezy room, Morton lighted a cigar and composed himself to read the manuscript in his usual lounging attitude. It interested him from the first sentence. The style was epigrammatic, and as sinewy as that of a Greek play. There was an ineffable poetic charm over the whole narrative, a quaint pathos in the dialect, and the actions of the humble characters, that charmed him inexpressibly.

Tears stood in his eyes when the story was finished. He sighed, rose impulsively, laid the manuscript on the table, and walked out on to the veranda.

Down in the yard a quaint lullaby was being droned by a negro woman over a sleeping child. From the end of the veranda he could see the row of cottages, and their inmates sitting before them. Lamplight showed through the

open door of one.   The lullaby died down, giving place to the faint mumbling of conversation.   A woman began to sing, and others
joined in.   Morton could not make out the
words, but the melody was beautiful.   A thousand regrets rushed over him.   Irene's story
reminded him of his mother's death.   He
recalled his father's grave, puritanical face,
and Lilly's spirituelle features.   He felt very
sad and lonely.

CHAPTER VIII.

NEXT morning Morton awoke from a tangle of conflicting dreams. The cocks were crowing in the yard below, birds were singing in the trees near his open windows.

The sun was shining brightly, and when he rose and looked out he was charmed with the view, over which a dim, gray atmospheric veil hovered. The grass was sparkling with blue, green, and gold dewdrops. The purple and pink clematis flowers, which climbed over the veranda, were wide open.

His first thoughts were of Irene's story. It was lying on the table and its beautifully written title-page looked at him reproachfully. He folded the manuscript carefully, and, going downstairs, strolled across the dewy lawn to a spot near the tall, white fence, where flowers, weeds, and bushes grew in riotous confusion. Three umbrageous magnolia-trees shaded a ramshackle summer-house, around which clustered a wilderness of flowers and plants.   Tiger-lilies dipped in dew, full-blown roses shedding their beauty, rosebuds just peeping from the green, and a mass of trumpet-flowers and love-vines gave fragrance to the air.

Sitting down in the summer-house he began to re-read the story.   Again its subtle power took hold of him.   Suddenly, without taking his eyes from the paper, he became aware that some one was looking at him.   He looked up.   Irene stood in the door of the latticed wall, a strange, breathless curiosity in her eyes.   She had recognized her manuscript.   In her mute bewilderment she appeared more startlingly entrancing than ever.   The white moon-flowers, lightly touching her uncovered golden hair, had sprinkled it with dewdrops.   Her arms were filled with fresh-cut flowers.

He dropped his eyes.

"I beg your pardon," he stammered, feeling his face grow hot beneath her unmelting look.

"It is mine, Mr. Dudley," said she in a tone of blended indignation and pain.

He made an ignominious failure of a smile.

"I cannot deny it," he returned, trying to meet her eyes.

" Where did you got it ? "

He hesitated, folding the crisp leaves of the manuscript a little awkwardly.

" Papa gave it you," she went on, almost bitterly. " He said something last night about wanting your opinion." ·

" I would not pain you for the world," said Morton, so earnestly and so gently that her features softened and her lashes began to quiver. " It has given me great pleasure to read it. It is a perfect story. It is——"

" Surely you read rapidly," she interrupted, a noticeable shadow of incredulity rising in her eyes.

" Sometimes I do," said he, failing to see her drift ; " but I have read this most carefully, I assure you——"

" But I saw you open it as I was coming across the grass a moment ago," she broke in, bending to pick a white thread from her gown, and crushing her flowers ruthlessly in doing so.

" Yes, but I read it last night," said he, " and I was about to—to enjoy it again."

He saw her struggle inwardly to prevent her gratification from going to her face. A dancing light enhanced the beauty of her eyes. Her complexion was as delicate of tint as the inner surface of the large conch shell which lay at her feet.

"Why do you encourage me so kindly?" she questioned, sinking into a seat opposite him and filling her lap to overflowing with her flowers.

"Because you have been too long without it," he said, sincerely. "This is really one of the finest character sketches I ever read!"

She could not reply at once. Her great trustful eyes filled with tears and she fell to trembling. He looked away from her, feeling his heart swell painfully.

"You are very kind, indeed; I can never forget what you have said;" she faltered, after a moment; "but do I not make a great many mistakes?"

"Not more than many well-known authors —not errors that an editor or proof-reader could not easily rectify. May I show you?"

Her eyes beamed a grateful consent.

He sat down beside her. She piled her flowers up at her side impulsively, looking very expectant; and as she moved up confidingly close to his side, he felt his heart bound wildly and then settle into a hot spot in his breast.

An indescribable blur, born of intense feeling, came before his eyes. He did not want to speak then, for he feared that she would detect his agitation in his voice.

He held the paper in front of her, and his hand rested upon hers, warm and responsive. She did not move it. She seemed to have no thought for anything save what he was to say. He had to struggle against a desire to throw his arms around her and clasp her to his breast, for something told him that she was giving him her heart without reservation, and that he loved her. She looked at him inquiringly, as if wondering at his delay. He took out his pencil. They bent their hands over the paper. Cupid, hidden among the flowers and vines, blew a single thread of her hair against his cheek, and it thrilled him from head to foot.

"See," said he, very tenderly, pointing to a line with his pencil. "Don't you see that you might have made this sentence stronger by forming two of it? So—may I?"

She nodded, and he quickly made a period of a comma, and capitalized a small letter.

"Oh!" she exclaimed, after he had read the two sentences with strong declamatory effect

—" oh! thank you; I see now, I shall never forget that! Here is another that has the same weakness."

She took the pencil and altered the text rapidly.

"You are right," said he; "how quickly you catch an idea!"

Then a shadow of reserve fell upon her. It occurred to her that she was speaking too freely with him, a great critic, about her humble efforts. He would not have looked at the story if her father had not given it to him. She grew almost rigid. The color in her face began to fade. She held out her hand for the manuscript, but he drew it beyond her reach, wondering at her sudden change.

" Give it to me, Mr. Dudley," she said, almost coldly.

" No," he returned, jestingly. " Your father and I purloined it from your desk in the dead of night; allow me to unburthen my soul by putting it back. In truth, I felt very guilty in that little study; it seemed sacred to me."

She did not return his smile, although her face softened. She gathered up her flowers, and, rising, started out of the door. He reached

her side in time to draw the damp vines out
of her path.

"Thank you," said she.

He caught her eyes. The rigid expression
was slowly melting from her mobile mouth.

"Well, we will put it back," said she, as they
walked side by side across the grass. "It is
really not worth notice or thought. It was all
papa's work. He always wants me to bow and
make my little speech to every stranger. But
I am truly grateful for your encouragement."

He told her he had done nothing to merit
her gratitude, and they went into the little
study together.

"It is so untidy," said she, raising the lid of
the desk; "throw it in with the rest."

He placed it carefully exactly where her
father had found it.

"Jane!" Irene called, to a little negro girl
who was sweeping the veranda, "come take
these flowers to mamma's room. Put them in
the jar near her lounge, in fresh water."

The scrawny-limbed black girl leaned her
broom-handle against a window-pane, and carried away the flowers.

"Here are some of my favorite books," said

Irene, brushing the dew from her white apron, and laying her garden-shears on the table, where "Transgression" peeped from a pile of others. "Most of these are by American authors."

Morton experienced a queer sensation. He wondered what he should say if she mentioned his books.

"Here is 'Free Joe' and some other tales by our own 'Uncle Remus,'" she went on. "Oh, I think Harris is grand! He gets my heart-strings in his grasp when I read his stories."

Morton could not formulate a reply, for her white hands were moving the books right and left. She picked up "Transgression" care-lessly and started to lay it down, but, as if actuated by a sudden thought, opened it.

"Did you ever read this, by Edgar Morton, a young Northern writer?"

He felt that he could not answer without embarrassment. He could not trust his lips even to the utterance of a monosyllable. He put his handkerchief to his mouth and coughed. She was waiting for a reply, her great, honest eyes on his face.

"Yes," he said, and coughed again.

He determined then to confess that he had written it; but she prevented him.

"It has been a study to me; I have read so much between the lines."

"What have you read between the lines?" he managed to ask, his tone sounding unnatural to him.

"Enough to sympathize with the author," said she, running her fingers through the leaves as if searching for some remembered passage. "He has great power, great genius: but in reading this book I was constantly haunted with the impression that he had two natures—a bad one and a good one. He moved me to tears at times; then again I could not help despising his characters, and feeling that he had made them like himself—weak and capable of deceit."

She looked up and was surprised at the cold gleam in his eyes and the tense expression of his face. He had resolved that she should never know who he was.

"Oh, what have I been saying?" she asked, in dismay. "Is the author a friend of yours, Mr. Dudley? I would not have spoken so for anything if——"

"No—no, not a particular friend," said he, exerting himself to crush down the bitterest mortification he had ever felt. At that moment he had not a hope.

"But you know Edgar Morton?" she asked.

"Yes, I have seen him—and talked with him—I can't say that I know him well." He shuddered, and avoided her trustful eyes.

The breakfast-bell began to ring out loudly. Judas, a little dwarfed negro boy with large feet and bow legs, was ringing it with all his might as he shambled through the hall.

"I shall not go in now," Irene said, putting the book down; "you know the way to the dining-room."

Her smile did not lift the weight which what she had said had put upon him; nor did the knowledge that she knew naught of his disguise lessen his discontent. The clatter of the boarders' feet as they hurried down the stairs and out to the dining-room grated harshly upon his nerves. His sky of hope, but yesterday so clear and bright, was now as dark as a pall. He was glad that Mr. Stanton was not at breakfast, and that the young men were too much engrossed over topics peculiarly their own to

note his silence.   He scarcely touched the food
that portly Aunt Millie set before him with
black, attentive hands.   He gulped down his
coffee so hot that it burnt his throat, and—
asking to be excused—rose from the table
before the others had finished eating.

He went out, crossed the weed-grown back-
yard, and passed through a gate into a wood at
the rear of the house.   Before him a little hill
rose gently.   He climbed to its summit through
a thick growth of young pines.   The top
reached, almost the whole of the little town lay
spread out before him.   The streets, bordered
with low buildings, neglected fences, and weed-
grown yards, looked as disconsolate as he felt.

He did not try to defend himself against
what Irene had so truthfully said.   He felt that
she was now beyond him forever.   He might
have confided in her—might have told her of his
disguise ; but it was now too late.   He could not
bear that humiliation.   He would go away soon,
return to New York, and marry the heiress.
After that he would forget the strange Southern
episode in his life.   He would not allow himself
to think of Irene Stanton.   He would forget how
he had held her in his arms that day on the

rock—no, that he could not forget, not as long as he lived.

Then he bethought himself that he owed Jean a letter, and he went slowly back to his room. He sat at the table a long time before he began to write. The letter was very short, for he was nervous. He told her that he was not feeling very well, which was the truth ; when he ended it, he was obliged to go over it again, for he had written very carelessly, omitted a good many letters and words, and had not expressed himself very coherently.

7

CHAPTER IX.

Days, weeks, a month passed by. Morton had lingered in the charming household much longer than he had expected. The boarders liked him, and enjoyed his stories of the North. He had won the hearts of the negroes by his liberality, and they were ever ready to do his bidding.

Old Uncle Tony was particularly attracted to the young stranger. Tony was an inveterate beggar, and seldom hinted to "Marse Dudley" that he wanted a dime without having a twenty-five-cent piece flipped at his woolly pate.

One bright day, Morton saw him mending a harness in the stable-yard, and paused to hear the old darkey talk. As he did so, and leaned over the fence near him, Tony was singing, "How firm er foundation de saints er de Lawd" with a good deal of satisfaction.

"Uncle Tony," said the young man, "are you a member of the Church?"

" Yesser, oh, yesser ! I reckon I is ; I done jine 'fo' de wah, en ergin atter de wah. He ! he ! En, Marster, ef de white folks git up er nurr fight 'twix um all, I reckon I jine de Chu'ch ergin."

" Why did you join again after the war ? Did you change your belief ? "

" No, suh," said Tony, scratching his deformed leg reflectively ; " no, suh ; but, yer see, de fus time, I went in ez er sort er beast er burden-lak fer de white folks, en I didn't spect ter git no front seat in de time ter come, en so I reckon I wuz er lill shackly wid my 'ligion. I des prayed w'en I felt lak it ; en didn't feel lak it much, kase, yer see, I 'low dat my marster will see I got thoo all right, kase dem times he wuz mighty watchful wid all us slaves. He wus sometimes even erfeard we gwine catch de fever fum' sposure, en all lak dat."

Morton laughed. " So you are more careful since you joined the last time. You haven't fallen from grace, have you ? "

" Marster, whut de use in you er talkin' ? Now you know nobody ain' gwine fall fum grace atter dey once git deh. Shuh ! you go 'long ! You never min' ! You cayn't fall

fum grace less'n you hat er mare name Grace,
en fall off'n 'er; dat de onlies' way, sho!"

"Tony," asked Morton, in a lowered tone,
"did you know that my time for leaving is drawing near? I can't stay down here always."

Tony's face fell. He raised his blue-black
eyes in slow surprise.

"Why, Marse Dudley, you ain' shorely
gwine pick up en go off," he said, regretfully.

"Yes," said Morton, touched by the old
man's tone; "yes, I must get back home pretty
soon."

Tony looked him directly in the face.

"Marse Dudley, den you is sho ter come back
ergin, I know."

"I don't know, Tony," returned Edgar, feeling a lump in his throat all at once; "I don't
know that my business will ever call me this
way again."

The serious expression of the old darkey's
eyes was mingled with a gleam of cunning.

"Shuh!" he grunted, "you cayn't fool dis
darkey, Marse Dudley; I done hat too much
dealin's wid young people. Y'all lak ter talk,
en talk, but suppen 'ight deh, Marse Dudley"
(laying his scrawny hand over his heart),

" suppin deh gwine fetch you ter dis house 'fo'
de sun set many times.   Whut 'bout my young
mistis, suh?   Oh! law! you ain' forgit 'er, I
know.   I'd des lak ter see de livin' man 'at
kin, atter he once laid eyes on 'er."

Morton felt his heart beat more quickly.
He looked away toward the little hill back of
the lot, a suspicious film gathering before his
vision.

" Marse Dudley," went on Tony, in a very
deep tone, in which there was a trace of husk-
iness, " I swar' you orter feel ez proud ez er
king, suh.   Now I'm er-gwine ter tell you suppin 'at I wouldn't tell no livin' soul 'cep' you,
en I wouldn't tell you but I see you des love
de ve'y groun' young miss walk on.   Oh, my!
you cayn't fool me; I done see it in yo' eyes
mo' times en I is got fingers en toes.   I done
seed you git white en flabby dat time w'en
you is made 'er fly up so on de front
po'ch er de big house w'en you 'low dat de
niggers wuz mistreat by some marsters lak
Unc' Tom wuz in his cabin, en so on.   I wuz
mighty sorry fer you, Marse Dudley, w'en I
see 'er flounce erway en lef' you all by yo'se 'f
'mongst de vines.   I don't know who Unc'

Tom wus, en who done tole you so much, bout
de strappin', but I boun' yo' young miss know
all erbout it; en I boun' yer dat nigger didn'
git mo'n he need.

"Well, I had my eye on you bofe all nex'
day, en, Marse Dudley, now, you did des look
awful! You look lak you mighter been sick fer
er mont', en you went mopin' roun' all dat
day. I didn't see young miss at meal times,
en so I kep' er watch out fer 'er. 'Twuz late
dat day w'en I seed 'er walkin' out to'ds de
hill back deh, en I lay fer 'er, I did. I made
out lak I wuz busy 'mongst de trees; en w'en
she come erlong so slow-lak in de dusky light,
I hope I mer die ef she didn't look lak er ghos',
she so white. She stopped at er rosebush, en
seem lak she wuz on de pint er pickin' er red
one er two, but she didn't, en des stood stark
still en look away off at de sky. Den she put
er hankercher up at 'er eyes en trembled lak
er leaf in er wind. She ain't see me, Marse
Dudley; but I knowed dat you en 'er wuz
bofe sick wid de same puny complaint.

"Well, dat same night, you know you is
call me up ter yo' room en give me er note fer
'er. I do know you seem lak yo' last hour

wuz ter han'. I know zactly what ail you, but
I never let on, en tuk de note up ter Miss
Inie. She wuz in 'er maw's room. Ole Miss
wuz ersleep on de bed, en she wuz settin'
at de winder, all by 'erse'f, mighty still en
squshed-lak.

"'What you want, Tony?' she say, 'dout
lookin' up. She is know me by de way dis 'ole
leg shuffle kerflipity flop—kerflipity-flop when
I walk.

"'I is fotch er letter fum Marse Dudley,' I
say; 'he des now ax me ter fetch it, en so he'p
me, Miss Inie, he certney is ve'y sick, en ef it
is fer any medicine, I kin tek it immegiate,
kase he do need 'tention.' (Tony hid a smile
with his long hand.)

"Marse Dudley, dat young lady des jump up
en mos' snatch de paper fum me, en she stood
at de table in de light er de lamp en read it; en
I hope I mer die ef she ain't bust out cryin'
over it. She turn her back ter me en stood
mighty still fer er long time. Deh wuzn't no
soun' 'cep' 'ole miss er-breathin'. Den terrectly
Miss Inie tun' roun', en we'n she speak, her
voice des ez shaky ez er flutter-wheel.

"'Yes,' she say, 'Tony, you kin say ter Mr.

Dudley dat I will grant his 'ques', en will be in de parlor in er few minutes, des ez soon ez I kin leave mamma!'

"But you know all dat, Marse Dudley—de ain't no use in me tellin' you, kase you know you bofe set up tell marster stopped it, kase it so late dat night, en tuk on lak two lill chillun over er new plaything. Dat de onlies fuss I ever seed up 'twix you, en I reckon dat ernough. Des one mo' day er dat en I do b'lieve you bofe 'u'd er been down in bed. Now, I reckon you won't come so spry ter dis yer nigger en tell yo' tales 'bout you is gwine off; en you never is gwine git back; en so on—en so on."

Tony was smiling with good-natured cunning, but Morton was silent. He turned away with a sudden determination to ask Irene to walk with him. And when she came tripping down the stairs to join him, looking so bewitchingly beautiful under her great black straw hat, he remembered Tony's words, and his heart went out to her. He was not demonstrative during their walk, though he did not lose a word of her talk, or allow one expression of her face to escape him. She was so beautiful—and so happy!

They strolled out into the meadows that lay beyond the town's ragged suburbs. He was tempted to throw himself at her feet and confess everything. Once he assisted her to cross a brook on the water-browned stepping stones. He took her soft, warm hand, and seemed to feel her life-blood pour into his veins. He held it for a moment after he had helped her across. She looked up into his eyes half questioningly, and blushed as she caught his strange, ardent glance. She drew her hand from his clasp, and became very silent, paying close attention to gathering wild flowers and grasses. She was wondering why he had never spoken of the love which intuition told her was hers. And he was thinking about Jean Wharton, and his duty to her, and his future. He decided once that he would give up the heiress and everything for the soulful girl at his side, but the memory of what she had said about the author of " Transgression " stole into his brain and banished the impulse. No he could not tell her who he was; it was too late; he must give her up; she would despise him. He knew now, beyond a doubt, that she loved him, and that when he went

away to return no more she would be unhappy.
But she would have to bear it. And he—well in
his active future life he might be able to put
her from his heart ; at any rate he would try.
He believed that he had enough honor not
to make her trouble any greater, so in a very
short time he would go. Then she would think
that he had not spoken because he did not love
her. But these reflections made him very miserable ; made him care very little for what the
future might bring. Somehow he could not
think of the future without her. That night
after leaving her he came to the conclusion
that Tony had known him better than he had
known himself.

One afternoon, shortly after this, while reading in his room, he noticed that the sky had
become so overcast with thick clouds that little
light entered the windows. The clouds thick-
ened and grew more threatening. Now and
then came an ominous roar of thunder. The
lightning began to flash in the dense clouds
in dazzling, zigzag shafts, which soon followed
one another in such rapid succession that the
whole black sky to the north seemed to reflect
the flames of some burning world.

Morton could hardly see twenty yards before him.   The tall trees on the lawn were enveloped in a gloom that moved along in murky spots like living shadows.   The long white fence came into view now and then like a mighty fallen pillar which had held the lowering firmament in place.   The wind rose.   Leaves and fragments of moss and bark rattled against the window-panes.   Clouds of dust loomed up from the streets and gave material density to the gloom.   The vines against the windows began to writhe and lash the glass furiously.   The trees with branches interlocked wrestled with one another in the fury of the blast.   A weeping-willow down by the walk gave its tender twigs and long leaves to the storm.

There was a dazzling stream of electricity; a deafening roar of thunder, a crash; and a giant oak near the house was shattered into a thousand pieces.   A heavy limb was hurled down upon the roof, and the very walls seemed to totter.   Loud cries of fear came from below. Morton dashed down the stairs.   In the sitting-room he found all the negroes gathered around Irene and her mother and her aunt.

Aunt Del was grovelling on her knees and

pleading to Mrs. Stanton to save her. Tony
sat trembling in a chair, his dilated eyes gleam-
ing in the dark like a cat's. A half dozen little
darkies sent up new and more deafening cries
with each blast that shook the windows.

"Marse Dudley!" gasped the fat cook, as
Edgar entered, "we all gwine be blowed up
dis time sho; dis is de Lawd's wuk!"

Edgar made his way to Irene, through the
excited throng, forcibly detaching the hands of
several clinging little negroes from her gown.
He had never seen her calmer.

"I am only concerned about mamma," she
said, raising her voice so that he could hear her
above the clang and clamor of storm; "she has
not been so well as usual to-day; this excitement is unfortunate for her."

"Don't fear for me, darling," Mrs. Stanton
joined in, making a trumpet of her thin hand.
"I am all right. There is not the least danger; the walls are very strong."

Morton ran to close a window which had
become unfastened. The rain fell in torrents.
Stones, pieces of timber, and shingles rattled
against the blinds, and the water streamed in
through broken window-panes.

Uncle Rastus, Aunt Del's husband, a long, slender negro, about fifty years of age, was kneeling in a corner praying.

"Good Lawd!" he groaned out, in jerky sentences, " des listen ter dat win'! Des listen how de sto'm is comin' down on sech er good 'oman ez ole Miss, en you ain't mek it let up! Fer Gawd's sake, Lawd, sen' dy mercy down ter tamper wid dis sto'm at once, en let us off safe! Lawd!" (as a sudden flash of lightning illuminated the room) " whut's dis?" And he sprang to his feet and stood quaking near his dusky wife.

Irene, seeing the pictures and curtains in the adjoining room blown about wildly, hastened thither to close a window. Morton followed her. The wind shut the door behind them with a loud slam, and they were alone together in the partial darkness. She had succeeded in lowering the window ere he could reach her, but as she turned back she ran into his embrace. Impulsively he closed his arms around her delicious form. He could not have helped it to save his life. She did not struggle, but turned and looked up into his eyes, her whole face illumined with love.

"I cannot help it, my brave darling!" he ejaculated. "I love you. I love you with all my soul!"

She made no effort to release herself from his arms, which tightened tenderly around her. Her eyes betrayed no great surprise, but they kindled with untold happiness. He drew her queenly head to his shoulder. He lowered his face and pressed his lips to hers, once, twice, thrice. Her hand met his in a warm, spasmodic clasp. In that contact with her lips he gave himself up to his love for her. He could only look at her transfigured face in a dazed sort of fashion, tingling in every fibre with ecstatic delight. Then he kissed her lingeringly, and tried to speak, but could not even whisper. A loud noise came from the adjoining room, and she moved away from him.

"I must go," she said, softly; and they went together toward the sitting-room.

He did not drop her hand till they were entering the door. He stood near Mrs. Stanton and Mrs. Livingston, and tried to assure them calmly that the worst of the storm was past, but the flame within him seemed to consume his words ere they reached his lips. Irene was telling Tony that there was no further danger, and as he joined his words to hers, he felt a delicious sense of ownership in her, and noted with ineffable delight, her softened manner as she turned to her aunt and her mother.

Irene stole away to her room upstairs to be alone with her emotions. She stood at a window and looked out at the murky weather. The rain beat in at a broken pane over her head, and shed a fine mist upon her, but she heeded it not. Her face was hot, and brightly aglow.

"He loves me! He loves me!" she murmured, over and over, to herself, as if she were talking in a dream. Gradually the skies grew yellow, the rain and wind ceased. An infinite calm settled upon the storm-swept earth. She went down, and walked round to the front veranda. Morton was there, eagerly watching for her appearance. Her eyes fell before the brightness of his face. She tried to meet him as she had so often done before, but she could not, besides, her aunt was standing on the veranda.

"Let's walk down to the gate," he said under his breath; and without a word she complied. In the west the sunset skies were purple, red and gold. They saw the branches of trees, which had been torn off by the storm, and the splinters of the shattered oak. A side fence was down. Streamlets ran gurgling across the lane.

" I am so sorry my favorite oak was struck." She sighed, but the sigh seemed belied by the glow in her cheeks. " And see, our retreat, the summer-house, is flat upon the earth."

After the evening meal, at which he had feasted his eyes upon her face in the lamplight, he got her shawl and followed her to the veranda, and there, in the dark, she allowed him to draw it gently around her. They sat for a half hour, silent and happy. The air was delightfully cool, and laden with the perfume of storm-beaten flowers. The moon rose and threw a mystic veil over the scene. They talked of the storm and the superstitious fright of the negroes, and laughed together, merrily. At last he put out his hand and ventured to take hers from the arm of her chair. She yielded it, and looked up into his face trustingly.

" Were you angry with me during the storm?" he asked, presently.

She dropped her eyes, and did not reply. He put his hand around her slender waist. She looked up ; in their blending gaze their spirits seemed to unite. He drew her into his arms.

"Were you angry?" he repeated, hardly knowing what he said.

"No," she replied, "not if you love me."

"Do you doubt it?" he asked, smiling.

"No, I could not doubt you in anything, for —for——"

"For you love me? Say it."

A bright, tremulous smile came over her face, but she did not speak.

"Tell me that you do!" he pleaded, his face very near her own.

She looked steadily into his eyes for a moment, then answered: "Yes, I do love you—very much."

Mr. Brown was playing a sacred melody on his flute, in his room. Little Judas, the dwarfed black boy, and his long, slender sister came up the walk, lugging between them a hamper-basket filled with splinters from the shattered oak. They paused to rest within a few steps of where the lovers sat behind the thick vines.

"Yes, en you des open yo' gap mouf en cry

8

lak er pig wid 'is liver-string cut w'en de sto'm come," said the girl. "En you mos' t'ar old Miss dress off'n her, you so bad skeerd."

"Who open dey mouf en cry, Miss?"

"You! dat's who, you lill ole squat frog!"

"Didn't!"

"Did!"

"Didn't!"

"Did! Come on, yer fool! I'll slap yo' chunk haid off ef you 'spute my wud!"

"Didn't cry," weakly defiant.

"DID!!!" at the top of her shrill voice; and she lifted her side of the basket five or six inches higher than his and jerked him along furiously.

"Didn't," very faintly, for he was trying to keep his end of the burden off the ground.

"Did-did-did-did-did-did-did-did-DID!" and they turned the corner, leaving the echo of the last feminine "did" ringing in the resounding hall.

The lovers laughed.

"That is prognostic of my fate in the future," he said, playfully. "I am little Judas, and you, Ca'line, will always have the last word."

She did not reply, and became very silent.

The remark reminded him of his engagement to Jean Wharton, and a damper fell on his happiness. He too became very quiet and thoughtful. He decided that he would write to Jean and ask for his release, and then he would confess everything to Irene and ask her to be his wife. Just then some one called Irene in the house, and, telling him good-night, she left him.

CHAPTER X.

MORTON started to his room. He wanted to think over a great many things. Brown's apartment was directly opposite to his, across the hall. The door was open, and Edgar could see him, flute in hand, at a table on which stood a shaded lamp and a music-book.

"Come in," said the musician, looking up; "come in and be sociable. When I have nothing else to do I stay at home and take things easy."

"I always know when you are here," said Morton, taking a chair; "for I can smell your tobacco across the hall and hear your music. You are, like myself, fond of smoking."

"Dudley," said Brown, laying his damp instrument upon the table, and filling his great pipe, "I declare you have a soft thing, with nothing to do but idle the time away here in this shady old place. I am sure I envy you your luck."

"But it is monotonous, sometimes," said
Morton, seeing the fellow's drift instantly.
"You know I haven't long to stay in the
South ; I must be getting home."

"Yes," said Brown, smiling in a knowing
way; "but when you do go, my dear fellow,
you'll leave the best part of yourself here."
He laughed, and rubbed his side-whiskers back
with his thin hands. "You see, Dudley, I've
known the fair angel of this house for a number of years, and, bless me ! if I ever knew a
man to see her, to know her, as you have done,
without falling head over heels in love with
her. It's only natural. I never thought of
her in that way myself, because I knew there
was no use ; but that girl has no equal on the
top of this earth."

"And you think," returned Morton, trying
to speak indifferently—"you think that a man
can't know her without losing his heart ? "

Brown smiled again. "He might, if he was
made out of stone or metal, but I don't think
you are, Mr. Dudley ; and, moreover, I think
you are cultivated enough to appreciate her,
and see what there is in her. Oh, she has had
matrimonial opportunities enough ; you need

not doubt that. Last winter, when she visited
her uncle in Atlanta, a rich young railroad
president fell in love with her, and followed
her home. I know that he wanted to marry
her, and I know that he got left; for I saw
him leaving the day she did him up. I never
saw such a face on a live man. Then there
was a banker in Macon, a handsome young
fellow, who used to come here to see her; but
he was served the same way. To tell you the
truth, Dudley, she really does like you better
than she ever has any of the others; that is
plain. I'm sure I wish you luck. But they
are awfully poor and hard run, and as proud
as Lucifer. The old gentleman has lost a great
deal of late. The man that takes her must
do his duty by the family; but who wouldn't
for such a girl?"

Morton was deeply interested, though he
half resented Brown's voluble familiarity. He
was glad when Tony came with his mail.

"Yer's some'n fer you, Marse Dudley," he
said, shambling into the room, his hat in one
hand and a bundle of letters in the other.

"All right, Tony," said Edgar, taking the
letters, and leaving Brown to his flute and pipe.

He went into his room to be alone.   After he had lighted his lamp, he sat for a long time at his writing-table, his letters unopened before him.   Brown's words had pleased him inexpressibly.   Irene had refused other men, men of position and of wealth, and she loved him. Then he began to look over his letters.   One was from Lang & Princeton, his publishers, stating that they were anticipating with pleasure the receipt of the MS. for his next work.

Another was from Jack Thornton, an intimate friend of his.

"Where are you, old chap?" it ran.   "I direct this in care of Lang & Princeton, hoping that it may reach you.   Wherever you are, my dear fellow, you ought to have burning ears, for you and your last affair are causing a good deal of gossip.   You know, of course, that Count Dartley is paying most devoted attention to Miss Wharton.   He is her shadow everywhere she goes.   And rumor says she has thrown you overboard, and that you, my poor broken-hearted friend, have skipped out to Europe to escape hearing of the matter.   All of which I do not believe.   Come home and tell us all about yourself. I congratulate you on the popularity of your literary work. I hear your name on all sides. Write! If you don't want me to know your hiding-place, date your letter 'Nowhere,' but by all means—write

"Yours, truly,

"JACK."

Morton flushed to the roots of his hair. He was vaguely angry. Of all things calculated to sting his pride he disliked nothing so much as being considered a rejected suitor. Could Jean be so foolish as to want to marry for a title? And yet he remembered that she had mentioned the count many times in her letters. He had been thinking about Irene so much of late that he had neglected the heiress badly.

He ran through the pile of letters, seeking one from her. He found one dated at Newport and opened it with suspense.

"MY DEAR EDGAR:" it said, "I really think that you have treated me shamefully. I do not intend to write you a long letter, because yours was so short. I suppose you are having a delightful time down there with your 'new friends.' I have a little piece of news for you. Uncle Eben, the Philadelphia merchant, died last week and has left me half-a-million dollars. I never knew him well, therefore I will not be hypocritical enough to pretend to be broken-hearted; but it was awfully good of him to remember me in his will.

"We have been having quite a gay time here, but we shall shortly return home. Count Dartley and his sister are with us, and it has been quite pleasant. You know I have never been fond of titled people, as a rule, but the count is such a true gentleman, and so unassuming! I know you would like him. Do you know, I have heard several times that he and I are engaged. How silly such reports are! But every girl is sure to have them circulated about her! More another time, dear Edgar.

"Jean."

Morton grew hot and cold by turns as he read and re-read the letter. He laid it down and walked to and fro in his room. To do him justice it should be said that in his excitement Irene was out of his thoughts. He could think of but one thing at that moment, and that was that Jean, whom he had so long regarded as his property, was falling in love with some one else.

He ground his teeth in mingled regret and anger. He convinced himself that he had been a fool in deliberately neglecting such a golden opportunity, and all on account of a beautiful girl who, after all, might not be necessary to his happiness. Had not Brown just spoken of her father's great financial straits? What right had he, a poor, moneyless author, to aspire to her hand. Had Irene at that moment stood before him in all her purity and loveliness he could never have written the letter that he wrote to Jean Wharton, he would have known himself too well.

He sat down to his typewriter. He was too excited to use a pen. Besides, Jean had once told him that she rather liked him to write to her on the machine with which he made his "copy" for publication, and he had occasionally humored her whim. Two sheets of writing paper, with a sheet of carbon paper between them, were ready for use on the roller. He had intended, that morning, to make a couple

of copies of a poem, but hearing Irene's voice
below, he had forgotten to begin the work.
He now saw only the outside sheet, and set to
work rapidly. When the letter was finished he
drew it from the machine with a metallic whir.
The carbon paper fell behind the table, and an
exact copy of the letter, on thin linen paper,
but unsigned, blew away unnoticed on to the
floor. While he was writing his name with a
pen, and addressing an envelope, the white curtains in the deep window embrasures stirred
and swelled inward. A sudden gust of air
blew out his lamp. The same agent of Fate
lifted the copy of the letter, and bore it
through the open door out into the hall;
thence it was wafted down to the floor beneath.

He folded and sealed the letter in the darkness, determined to walk down to the post-office
and mail it. He wanted to get it off his mind.
He intended to keep his promise to the heiress.
He had not yet asked Irene to be his wife. He
had simply told her that he loved her, and he
had spoken the truth. Early in the morning
he would tell her that he was engaged to another. Then he would pack up his things and
go away.

As he passed down the stairs into the dimly-lighted hall, he observed little black Judas sitting in a corner, evidently waiting for some one. The little fellow had a sheet of paper in his dusky hands, but Morton did not give it a thought. After he had passed out into the yard, he looked back through the hall and saw a light in Irene's study. Her shadow was outlined on the wall of the little room, but he could not see her face, although he stood for several minutes, waiting and hoping to do so. But even her shadow affected him; and as he lingered under the white arching lintel of the tall front gate, he took out the letter to Jean and started to tear it up, whilst a reckless happiness shone for an instant on his face. But something stayed his fingers; he hesitated for a moment, then put the letter into his pocket, and went slowly on to the post-office.

CHAPTER XI.

" Whut dis, Miss Inie ? "

It was Judas's low voice at the corner of Irene's desk. He held a type-written sheet before her, his grimy fingers soiling its whiteness.

She recognized it at a glance as Morton's work. He had once brought the machine down into the parlor to show it to her. The first words at the top sent a hot flush to her face :

" My own darling."

She put out her white hand and took the paper.

" It is mine," she said. Then, " Where did you get it, Judas ? " Her voice was tremulous with ineffable delight.

" I pick it up out deh in de hall, I did, Miss Inie. It flew down fum up-sta'rs, I reckon, kase it lit flop on top my haid ez I wuz des drappin' off ter sleep."

" It is mine," she repeated, and she waited an instant for him to go away.

But something in her unusual excitement of

tone and her facial brightness kept him. She forgot Judas, fastening her eager eyes again on the paper. He had written to her because he had not had the courage to speak plainly. He had called her " darling." But as she read on, the color left her cheeks, the light of joy died out of her eyes. She looked like a statue of old ivory crowned with tresses of living gold. Her head sank toward the letter :

" My own Darling :—How glad I was to hear from you ! So, by your uncle's death you are now even more wealthy. Jean, dear, you can't imagine how it pains me to feel that we are so unequal in the eyes of the world. You know I have always felt it, and I shall now feel it more than ever. I am jealous of Count Dartiey. I know he is in love with you. Just think of all you are giving up for a poor moneyless, struggling mortal ! I shall not be here long now. I shall soon return to you. It is late at night, and as my lamp is giving a poor light, I am hammering this out to you on my faithful machine. You will pardon me, I know. I will write you a long letter to-morrow. Good-b---

" Yours ever "

There was no signature. Irene knew that he signed his type-written letters with a pen. She looked up. Judas was standing at the end of the desk, his black face glistening in the light, his eyes holding a questioning expression. The little fellow shrank before her stony look, and took his hand from the desk.

"Judas," said she, in a voice that was very husky, "go away. Do not stay here."

His bare footsteps slurred like weird, echoing whispers in the empty hall, and then died on the grass of the lawn. Irene's head sank lower and lower, till her face was in her hands upon the desk. She remained in that motionless position for a long time.

Morton, returning, came up the walk, and still seeing the light in her room, paused at the veranda. But when she had bowed, her shadow had disappeared from the wall, and he supposed she was no longer there. All the way from the post-office he had looked forward to seeing at least her shadow again before he retired. And yet he had thought that he could forget her in a few months.

Irene heard and recognized his walk. She raised her head, and listened to his step as he

ascended the stairs. She looked ten years
older. The creases of her hands had moulded
wrinkles in her cheeks. There was a cold, steady
gleam in her eyes. She rose and put the letter
into her desk. She blew out her lamp, but
remained in the darkness trying to collect her
thoughts. Then she groped back to the desk,
and, securing the letter, put it into her bosom.
She stood still, looking out through the hall into
the moonlight on the lawn. Her limbs seemed
to have lost their power, and she dragged
herself with painful slowness through the
house and upstairs to her mother's room.
Mrs. Stanton had been worse that day. The
lamp was burning low. The porcelain lamp-
shade threw on the wall a huge cone-shaped
shadow with a quivering thread of light through
it. The girl turned up the wick a little, and
shrank back suddenly as the oil gurgled through
the tubes.

The town clock was striking eleven. Irene
looked at her mother. The thin, white features
were wrapped in sleep. Going to the mantel-
piece, she took down a vial containing a white
powder, and shuddered convulsively. She
glanced across the room to her mother's shaded

face, shook out a little heap of the powder upon a piece of paper, and put it into a wine-glass on the table, poured some water upon it and stirred the mixture with a tiny silver spoon.

The moon came out from behind a cloud and threw her pathetic rays through a window. Irene held the thin glass between her and the lamp to see if the powder had dissolved; then she softly moved to her mother's bed. Seating herself in a chair, she waited for Mrs. Stanton to wake. In a few moments the invalid opened her eyes.

"Mamma, you must take your medicine now; the doctor said at half-past ten, and it is after the time."

Mrs. Stanton smiled faintly and fell asleep again.

The girl raised the gray head upon her arm. The blue eyes opened wider; a dreamy smile flitted across the wrinkled face. Irene held the glass to the half-parted lips. The invalid swallowed unconsciously. The daughter turned the hot pillow over, and laid her mother gently down. Then she disrobed herself.

She knelt in the moonlight, at the side of the bed, looking very white and faint. The

9

moments passed. Not a word escaped her lips. Her prayer was only a mute sacrifice of all her hopes, aspirations and dreams, which she was bringing to God's altar to exchange for hopeless realities. She had intended, when she knelt, to speak to Him of her trouble, but she only thought over it all, and uttered no complaint.

But though she had not gone to God, she did want to confide in her mother. She got into bed and nestled close to the sleeper, willing to fancy that she was a child again. But her mother was in a deep, unnatural slumber, and did not stir. The doctor had said that Mrs. Stanton might not wholly recover her reasoning powers, and, as Irene thought of never having her mother's entire sympathy in her overwhelming trouble, the last spark of desire in her breast expired.

She twined her arms with inexpressible tenderness around the sleeper, who did not wake. The girl's grief grew wild. She raised her face over her mother's, and kissed the half-opened mouth gently, so as not to disturb her.

"Oh, mamma, darling!" she said, softly, "you must love me as you used to do, for you

are all—all—all I have in the wide world—oh,
I am so lonely!"

Mrs. Stanton moved slightly.

"What is it?" she asked, half asleep.

The girl did not speak, but lay breathlessly
still, hoping that her mother would not fully
awake.

"What is the matter, my pet?" Mrs. Stanton asked, turning on her side, and throwing
her arms around her child.

"Nothing, mamma dear; I was—was dreaming; I am sorry I woke you. Go back to
sleep. I am all right."

Her voice faded into the stillness. She
turned and looked out of the window into the
peaceful night. She lay there for hours in a
deathlike calm, not daring to stir for fear
of waking the slumberer—thinking, thinking,
thinking, with a crushed heart in her breast.
Toward day, when the sky in the east had
grown gray, she dropped to sleep.

CHAPTER XII.

THAT night Edgar Morton hardly closed his eyes. The thought of giving Irene up lay like a heavy weight on his breast.

He arose early in the morning and went immediately down, hoping to meet her; but he saw nothing of her, and his hopes sank when Mr. Stanton told him that Irene seemed a little unwell, and was loath to leave her mother's room. Breakfast over, Morton went out, feeling abjectly miserable. Irene was not well. He had never felt so wretched. Could he possibly give her up—go away, to see her no more, and let her think him dishonorable—untrue—unworthy of the love she had so trustingly given him?

"No!" he said to himself, "I'd rather die than to leave her—I love her more than my soul. I will tell her everything, and beg her forgiveness."

He strolled on over the dewy grass till he came to the summer-house which had been rebuilt.

The grass muffled his steps, so that Irene, standing behind a young cedar, her hand resting on the framework of a grape-vine, did not note his approach. He started with surprise at seeing her so unexpectedly, and went toward her impulsively. But when she turned her face to him, he paled to the lips. He stood before her, too surprised to speak, his intended words of greeting dying before they reached his lips.

She was as pale as death. Lines of suffering lay about her tightened mouth; purple curves shaded her great, scornful eyes. She looked beautiful, imperious.

"Good-morning, Mr. Dudley," said she, in such a calm, unruffled tone, and with such a stern, unrelenting stare, that his heart sank in dismay.

"Your father told me you were unwell," he managed to stammer, almost dumb from dawning fears as she turned her awful eyes away for an instant; "but really I did not expect to see——"

"To see me looking quite so unpresentable," she interpolated, ironically; "but you know, Mr. Dudley, that, after all, we women are only women; nothing more. Very slight things affect us, I assure you."

"Irene," he gasped, "what is the matter? Why——"

She held up one white hand with an imperative gesture, and his words dwindled away into nothingness. She smiled as coldly as the reflection of sunlight from an iceberg. Her features were so rigidly ghastly that he grew weak in fearful suspense.

"Please reserve your platitudes for some one else," said she, with so sharp a tone, and such a frozen look, that he read unutterable contempt in them both. "I do not feel in the humor to listen to them. My mother was so ill last night, I—suppose I lost too much sleep; I——"

"Irene, you do not love me!" he groaned. "I have never seen you this——"

"I do not love you!" she broke in, coldly, contemptuously. "Well, it doesn't matter! But pardon me—I have something of yours, which I want to return to you. It is only a copy, I believe, but I presume that all systematic business men keep some sort of record of their correspondence, and you may wish to file this. Men are very progressive in the present day. Do you keep a copy of all your *written* words of love ?" She put a quivering hand into her bosom and handed him a crumpled sheet of paper. His face showed unguarded surprise as he opened and recognized it. He stared at her helplessly. A faint glimmer of a smile touched her rigid lips as she bent and plucked a pink rose and fastened it in her hair. He was about to speak, but she raised her hand again.

"Not a word !" A look of obstinate determination emphasized her command. "If you would have me entertain the slightest respect for you, do not attempt to deny or explain. Say nothing. I will not listen. I never want to hear it mentioned. I *will* have my way in this !"

Had his life depended on his utterance he could not have spoken at that instant. Her great suffering did not escape him, as she stood trying to steady herself, her fingers tightly screwed and intertwisted.

"I have but one wish, Mr. Dudley, and I know that you will grant it. I feel, despite what has passed, that you possess some true gentlemanly instincts. I should dislike to think that even my father, who likes you, could be so deceived in appearances. I am not very strong, and as my mother is seriously ill, I should like for you to go away. Of course, I do not mean from G—— ; but there are other houses in town where you can stay. I have deliberated over this, and I assure you it has cost me a struggle to speak of it. If I alone were concerned it would be different ; but my mother needs me now all the time, and I could not be—be to her as I should, unless—unless you are away. You may think me weak, and that I lack pride in confessing so much now ; but I have never met a thorough man of the world before, and I little understand how a society woman should deport herself when she finds herself—mistaken. Some women would, no doubt, pretend to care nothing about it, and laugh at it all as a joke, but I cannot affect anything. I confess, without shame, that I loved you. Why should I deny it ? It is all over with now. If you will go—at once—I can do my duty better. I can better attend to my mother's needs when you are not here to remind me how very child-like I have been. I think you will understand, and—and will grant my wish. That is all."

She gathered up her skirt with a poor, trembling hand, and turned from him. Had his heart been torn out before his eyes and ground beneath her feet he could not have suffered more.

" Irene, have mercy !" he groaned, his eyes dilating with the wild passion of his yearning ; and he flung himself on his knees upon the damp grass.

But she did not look round. He rose and tottered along a few steps after her, but the vines and low-hanging foliage hid her drooping figure ; he sank upon a bench as weak as an infant.

"Irene ! Irene !" he muttered, "have mercy ! Have mercy !"

He sat very still for several moments, trying to collect his thoughts. Something told him that he was powerless to change matters. Had he confessed all before she read the letter, she might, in time, have forgiven him,

but now a full explanation would only make
her hate him the more. Something whispered
to him : "Go away at once. She does not
know who you are. She can never know. In
the future, by the aid of Jean Wharton's
money and your genius you will become great
and she will read your works with admiration,
and never suspect that she once knew Edgar
Morton. Go, for you can never win back her
confidence and love."

A mocking-bird was piping sweetly in a tall
poplar tree. The red brick of the old mansion
showed through the foliage, and beyond rose
the serried pines of the hill, clearly outlined
against the sky. Morton rose, feeling as one
does after a long illness, and slowly made his
way across the lawn. He staggered against a
tree, shaking down a shower of dew into his face.
The veranda and the hall were empty. An air
of solitude pervaded everything. No sound
was heard save an occasional clatter of dishes
from the kitchen. It was almost a relief to
see Aunt Del come out into the yard and hang
a rug across a side-fence to sun. He went upstairs into his room and threw himself on his bed.

His throat was dry, his brain on fire. Then,

all at once, he realized that he had no right to be there, since Irene had asked him to go. He got up and went to his mirror. He could hardly believe that the ghastly image was his own. He put his chin upon his quivering hands, with his face close to the glass, and looked at himself steadily. Presently he went to the table and wrote to Irene:

"Miss Stanton,—I have sacrificed the right to call myself your friend. I have deceived you in some things, but as I hope for immortality, I love you with all my soul. Let me see you only once to confess all. I have been weak, but I love you, and cannot live without your forgiveness."

He did not sign it. He did not want to use his assumed name again, and he preferred to tell her his own to her face. Looking from the window he saw Judas playing in the yard below, and called to the boy to come up. He met the slow-moving dwarf on the stairs, and gave him the note to take to his young mistress. Morton paced the floor in half-frenzied impatience, counting the seconds till he heard the boy's bare feet on the steps. He went half-way down

the stairs to meet him. The note was his own,
returned; but, written on its margin in Irene's
clear hand, he read:

"I can only renew my request. I will never
see you again. I have told my father that
you are called away. This is my only and
last request, and, believe me, I tremble when I
think that you may delay in granting it. I feel
that I have a right to make it, *even to demand*
your compliance.　　　IRENE STANTON."

Judas stood looking at him with inquisitive
eyes, holding a top-string between his shining
teeth and one of his flat feet resting idly upon
the other.

"Wait a moment, Judas," said Morton,
huskily.

He almost fell into the chair at the table.
His hand trembled as if it were palsied, as he
wrote:—

"I am all in the wrong. I go at once. I
hope soon to be able to justify myself—in part,
at least. But I will not trouble you now.
Good-bye."

He deliberated for an instant, as to whether he should sign his own name, then he sent it unsigned, telling himself that he would soon write her a full confession.

Two hours later he stood on the veranda bidding Mr. Stanton good-bye. Tony and another negro were putting his luggage into a dray. A group of negroes stood at the corner of the house. They all looked sad. Morton had few words to say as he went among them and shook their honest hands. Tears were in the eyes of the older ones, for they all loved him.

"Marse Dudley, suh," said Aunt Del, as she wiped her chubby hands on her apron, "we is gwine ter miss you er mighty heap. De ain't been one nice white gen'man yer in er long time lak you, suh, en I'm er gwine sen' up er prayer fur you night en mornin'. You is in trouble. I kin see dat; en ef you is los' any yo' folks, I'm mighty sorry fer you, en Gawd bless you!"

Mr. Stanton's kind old eyes glistened a little as he went down the long walk at Morton's side.

" Mr. Dudley, we regret very much to lose you," he said, with deep feeling. "We have come to regard you as one of our circle, you know, and we shall miss you. You must not forget us, and must come again to see us ; rest assured, you will always be welcome."

In his excitement Edgar had forgotten that he had not paid for his last month's board. And when he suddenly remembered it, and held the money toward Mr. Stanton, the old man put up his hand to push it back.

" No," he said, " let us consider you as our guest for this last month. I should like to have it so. We have enjoyed many a talk together. At my age I meet few men who interest me as you have done."

Morton's face paled to the roots of his hair. He almost forced the money into the old man's palm. His tone surprised Mr. Stanton.

" Oh, no, I could not ! I really could not ! " he gasped.

" Well, well, have it your way," said Mr. Stanton. " Good-bye. My wife sends her best wishes, and regrets that she is not well enough to see you before you go. But you will leave me your address, I might want to write, you know."

Without thinking of what he was doing, Morton wrote it on the paper Mr. Stanton held toward him.

"Then you go to New York?" asked the old man, surprised.

Morton's eyes fell; his trouble had been so great that he had lost sight of the part he was playing.

"Yes, that will be my address," he stammered, turning away.

As he went down the long street, Edgar turned to take a last look at the place which he had learned to love so dearly. Everything was absolutely still about the house; the branches of the trees were motionless. Aunt Del stood in the kitchen door, a huge dish-pan under her arm, looking after him. Little Judas sat on an inverted wash-tub in the yard, swinging his feet back and forth. The veranda was empty. He saw the very vines and trellis behind which he had held Irene in his arms; and, as the old house vanished among the mantling trees, he felt like a homeless wanderer on the face of the earth.

To avoid meeting any one he knew, he went to the station by way of a back street. The

continual blur before his eyes was so blinding
that he could hardly see his way. As he took
his seat in the train, it seemed to him that he
was leaving his very soul behind him.

When Mr. Stanton turned back into the
house, he found Irene, reclining on a lounge
in the sitting-room. Noticing that the curtains
of a window looking toward the town were
moving slightly, though not the faintest breeze
was astir, the idea struck him that she had been
at the window and had suddenly thrown herself
on the lounge on hearing his footsteps.

"Irene, pet," said he, gently—and he drew
a chair near the lounge and sat down,—"I
am sorry Dudley has gone. He certainly loves
you, my child, with all his heart. I really
think you ought to have suspected it all along,
and to have broken with him before this, since
you have evidently decided not to accept
him."

She looked up into her father's eyes and
tried to smile indifferently.

"Papa," she answered him, pitifully smooth-
ing out the crumpled skirt of her gown, and
trying valiantly to steady her twitching lips—
"papa dear, you men expect so much of us.

I assure you that I acquainted Mr. Dudley with the state of my feelings as soon as I learned what his intentions were with regard to me. You see "—and for an instant she gripped her throat with a quivering hand,—"you see, he did not let me know—at once."

"And you did not love him, then, dear?" said the old man, bending over her and toying with the hair about her brow.

A cold sweat stood on her face. She tried to force the smile to her mouth again, but only a pitiful grimace came to her distorted features. She flung up her arms suddenly and drew the white head down, to hide her struggle; but when his lips touched hers, she tightened her arms around his neck and burst into a passion of tears.

10

CHAPTER XIII.

THE winds of September, a trifle more destructive than those of August, were cutting off some of the red and gold leaves from the trees that shaded the Stanton residence. The grapes were ripe and purple, the fig-trees laden with sun-cracked and honey-coated fruit, when Mrs. Stanton died.

It is painful to stand by the bedside of a loved one and see a life pass away; to see dear eyes lose the light of recognition in the strange, new current of inexplicable change; to bend longingly, awe-stricken with a sense of profound mystery, over the last of what represented so much to our bereaved senses; to feel, in the cold, irresponsive hand, that it is mere mockery to turn thither for solace.

Irene stood at her mother's death-bed with her father and aunt, a bewildered stare of agony in her eyes. At the foot of the bed were the negroes. Aunt Del, her head turbaned in white; Uncle Tony, stick in hand, stood by Uncle Rastus. Aunt Millie held the hands of two little colored girls. Judas sat on a hassock, his hands crossed in his lap, his pockets bulging with forgotten playthings, an unfathomable expression on his face.

A harrowing, breathless moment of suspense, then all was over. Tears had stolen from Aunt Del's eyes and lay sparkling on her dusky cheeks. She moved in a mute, slipshod way among the children, and signed to them to go quietly down the stairs. Uncle Tony hobbled away with a soft tread that was pathetic.

Mrs. Livingston led her tearless niece into an adjoining room and sat down beside her. She pillowed the troubled head upon her breast, but spoke not a word. Mr. Stanton, who had lingered a moment over his wife's body, turned from the room. He came to Irene and held out his arms to her in mute appeal. She went to him. He did not press her to his breast as she thought he would, but held her face between his hands, and gazed searchingly into it for a moment, then, releasing her, went quickly from the room.

"He always said I looked like mamma," said

Irene, as her aunt took her into her arms again.

Then she hid her face, for she thought she was going to shed tears, but she did not.

$\cdot$ $\cdot$ $\cdot$ $\cdot$ $\cdot$ $\cdot$

. After her mother's death, Irene never spoke of her absent lover to her father, and tried to put him altogether out of her thoughts. Her memory of him was sorrow-clouded—fraught with humiliating pain. She associated him with the life that had come before her greatest grief, believing, poor girl! that all her weight of woe was caused by the loss of her mother. In everything about the house she found the reminder of a past joy. It gave her some comfort to minister to her father's wants, but her pale face and sunken cheeks still testified to the anguish within.

While Mr. Stanton was at his place of business she felt the awful solitude of her life with redoubled force. Soon financial adversity added its sting to the grief of the inmates of the stricken house. Since his wife's death the old man had made some new mistakes in investments, and suddenly found himself on the brink of ruin.

Irene read his trouble in his eyes, and cudgelled her young brain to devise a plan to aid him. One day it flashed upon her to try to sell some of her literary work. With a vigor born of despair, she set to work to write a novel. She put her whole soul into the work. She made a few of her characters experience something like the grief she felt while writing the story, and gave to others the joy which had been her portion in the past. When her work was finished, something told her that she had done well, that there were sympathetic souls in the world who would read her story with some of the feeling that had dimmed her eyes as she wrote it.

The day when she carefully tied up the little packet, and secretly took it to the post-office, was an important one in her life. She sent it, as chance would have it, to Lang & Princeton, New York. That night at the supper-table she searched her father's care-worn face anew, and in the quiet of her study, a few moments later, she earnestly prayed that through the work she had just sent away she might be able to aid him.

The negroes were not unaware of the new

cares which had fallen to the lot of their master, and were deeply sympathetic, though Tony was, perhaps, the truest and most concerned of all. He often bewailed his master's misfortune, and tried to devise a plan to assist him.

One day the old darkey saw a lawyer enter the house and remain in close conference with his master for several hours, and he hung about the front veranda very much distressed till he saw the visitor depart. He had heard it whispered among the negroes that the old homestead was about to pass into alien hands. After the lawyer had gone, Tony limped across the yard into his cottage. He went to an old chest in a corner, unfastened a key from a string round his neck, and, unlocking the massive padlock, he slowly raised the lid. He took out a small tobacco-bag almost filled with coin, and shook it till the contents jingled, and smiled and slyly chuckled to himself. He turned away, leaving the chest unlocked for the first time for years, went back to his master's house, and slowly made his way through kitchen and dining-room, his crooked leg swinging in a disjointed fashion from side to side, his heavy

cane thumping on the floor. Aunt Del and
Aunt Millie looked at him, saw his money-bag,
and wondered. On reaching the door of the
sitting-room, where Mr. Stanton sat at the fire,
smoking a pipe, having given up the luxury of
cigars, Tony rapped gently.

"Come in!"

"Well," as Tony, shame faced, tattered hat
in hand, entered, "what is it?"

"Marster," in trembling notes, "marster, I
is yer um all talk en talk 'bout you is gwine
hatter 'linquish dis yer home-place en all—en—
en, marster, 'scuse me,"—tears were in the blue-
black eyes beneath the stubbly brows—"but,
marster, I kin stan' mos' anything 'cep' dat."

"Well, what of it?" the master answered,
with a sigh from his heart. "Adversities must
come to us all, Tony?"

"Marster,"—and Tony shook his bag of
money gently—"Marster, I is been layin' by er
lill fer er long time, mighty nigh ever sence
de wah. I des got in dis lill poke edzactly
forty-fo' dollars en fifteen cents. En, marster,
I want you ter tek it ter he'p you out, suh."

Mr. Stanton looked up at the black face
with a sudden start, then turned his head away.

"Hang your impudence, you black rogue!"
he exclaimed, facing the old darkey and trying
to pretend to be angry. "I'll thrash you if
you come to me with any of your sympathy!
I don't want your money!"

Not a quiver disturbed Tony's gaunt face,
nor did he lower so much as the breadth of a
hair his outstretched hand, in whose clutch lay
the coin-filled tobacco-bag.

"Des forty-fo' dollars an' fifteen cents!" he
repeated, firmly—"some dimes, some nickels,
er few Mexicans wuth eighty-five cents a-piece,
mebby mo', er five-dollar gol' piece, suh, en er
good many halves en dollars, en so on; en what
is mo', Mr. Linkum owes me yit fer de white
shote he got dat time."

There was a silence for a few moments. It
was a picture worthy of the brush of highest
genius. Tears stole into the white man's eyes,
humbleness and entreaty lay in the black's.
The master smiled in an unnatural, poorly-
affected way as he fumbled in his pocket for
his handkerchief.

"Put up your money, Tony, you old thief.
Ha! ha! ha!" he laughed, through his tears;
"you know I always told you you could not

keep from stealing chickens; but now, you black rascal, you are trying to get me to go in cahoot with you, and share your spoils. No, siree, Bob! you can't work that trick on me, old fellow; I wouldn't have your chicken money. Besides—" he grew very serious, lowered his voice, and wiped his eyes surreptitiously, " besides, I don't need it. I've got a month to raise that little amount in, and I will get it somehow, by hook or crook. Now go, Tony."

The old negro seemed to deliberate with himself whether he should say anything more. He raised his money-bag a little and shook it slightly, but that was all.

" Yes, suh; yes, suh," he said, as he began to withdraw.

" Tony!" The old negro was softly closing the door behind him.

" Suh? yes, marster!" and a black, grinning face was thrust in at the door, and the money-bag expectantly extended.

" Tony, you said once that you wanted a horse to hitch to that little wagon of yours with the ' whopity ' wheels, as you call them. I've got that slow old plug, Jack, in the stable,

and have no earthly use for him. Tony, consider him a gift from me. I don't approve of
your thieving traits, you old rascal, but the
horse is yours, you hear ? "

" No, suh, I don't yer ; I don't want no
hoss ! " vigorously, almost indignantly ; " who
say I is want er hoss? I don't need no hoss ;
en w'at's mo', I ain't gwine hat no hoss, now
you yer me once en fer all ! Shuh ! what is got
in yer, I wonder ?"

Tony tottered off home, muttering to himself,
and the old white man bent over the fire, and
held a damp, steaming hand over the hot
ashes.

CHAPTER XIV.

On the evening of the day he reached New York, Morton called to see Jean. His mind was filled with deep melancholy, and a burthen of unspeakable remorse rested upon him. He wanted to write to Irene, but would not do so till he could tell her of his release from his promise to the heiress. He had determined to tell Jean all, and to appeal to her for advice in his trouble.

"Oh, my!" Jean exclaimed in dismay, as she entered the drawing-room to greet him. "Can this be you? Wh—why, Edgar, have you been ill?"

Then, before he could reply, she went into the hall to tell the servant that she was at home to no one. She returned with a grave face and sat down near where he was standing. She did not seem to notice that he had not kissed her, and that his hand-shake lacked its usual warmth. She was looking sadly into his thin, wan face.

"Have you been ill, Edgar?" she repeated, anxiously.

"No," said he, awkwardly, "but I am rather tired from my journey."

Silence filled the room. She did not look at him with her old directness. She was evidently not satisfied with his reply to her question.

"Edgar," said she presently, in a tone that went to his heart, "you are in trouble; I don't know what it is, but it must be great. Tell me the straight truth, no matter what it is—no matter if it separates us for the future. Tell me everything! You are too true, too great by nature, to deceive me in anything—tell me!"

He looked down into her eyes. They had once seemed unattractive to him, but they now shone with rare beauty of soul. His heart felt lighter.

"Tell me all," she went on; "keep back nothing; I tell you you could not surprise me now!"

He was standing near the fireplace. Amid a tangle of evergreens, a mock fire threw a blood-red glow on to the tiles at his feet. He leaned against the cabinet-mantel, and, as she spoke, quivered from head to foot. He wanted to tell her how he was suffering, and that he had made a mistake in promising to marry her. He looked down at her; her hands were crossed; she was waiting anxiously for him to speak.

"Jean," he said, "I once told you that I loved you——"

"And you do not now, Edgar; well, go on," she said, tightening her lips. "Perhaps you never did; we often do not understand ourselves. But we will pass that; tell me all— everything!"

He was silent for a moment, then reading her kind, womanly face with rising hopes, he concluded:

"No, I do not love you—as—as I should, to make you perfectly happy."

Rid of his burden, he stood looking at her with a glance that was most pitiful.

"Edgar," said she, making room for him at her side, on the divan, "come, sit by me."

He obeyed.

"Now, tell me all about it, from the first moment you saw her. She is Southern, and beautiful, and—and I know she is clever, and that you both are congenial in your tastes."

He tried to smile in his old deceptive way, but the effort was a failure.

"She is all that and more," he answered, abashed.

He said nothing more for several minutes. But as the true woman at his side continued to encourage him, as kindly and tenderly as a sister might have done, he told her the whole story, and reserved nothing.

"Edgar," said she, with a deep-drawn sigh, when he had finished—"Edgar, you never could have loved me that way, and I am afraid I could never care for you as I fancy she does. I confess that I have been very foolish. To be perfectly truthful, I acknowledge that I did not love you with all my heart. I think I was interested in you more than in any other man, because I was so proud of you, and hoped—fancied—that you could love me as ideally as your heroes love in your stories." She was silent a moment, looking thoughtfully at the carpet, then she said : "It would have been a great mistake for us both. You must marry her. I would give all I possess to enjoy, even for a brief period, such happiness as is in store for you two."

His face took on a radiance that made him look almost boyish. He threw his arms around her and kissed her impulsively.

"Now, that will do," she said, quietly, and drew herself away. "Once is enough, you great boy; but, then, we are such good friends."

Later in the evening she spoke of the Count, and shyly confessed that she really liked her new lover; he had been so kind, and was such a perfect gentleman. He was even then pressing his suit.

"You know, Edgar," she said, "I did not want to tell him of our engagement, so what was I to do?"

"Do you think he could make you happy?"

She smiled and blushed slightly. "I enjoy his society very much; he is fond of many things that I like."

Before he slept that night, Edgar wrote a long letter to Irene. He confessed everything. He told her his real name; that he had been tempted to marry a wealthy woman, but, having met her and loved her with all his soul, that he **could** never think of anyone else as his wife.

Then he closed by saying that Miss Wharton had willingly released him from his engagement and was to marry another, and implored her to write him her forgiveness.

Ten days passed, and no reply came. She despised him, he said to himself; she would never forgive him.

One day his landlady called him to give him his mail.

"By the way, Mr. Morton," said she, as he was turning away, "can you tell me who Mr. Marshal Dudley is? There is a letter here with that name upon it. It may be for some one who intends to stop with us."

For an instant Morton lost his self-possession.

"It is for me, Mrs. Long," he said, excitedly. Then he looked very confused.

"For you?" asked the woman, surprised.

"Yes," pulling himself together. "Of course, it is not my name, but I used it once. The letter must be for me."

Mrs. Long went into another room and brought it to him.

"Oh, you authors!" she exclaimed playfully, shaking the letter at him. "You are a queer lot. This is one of your tricks, I'm sure!"

He took the letter and turned up the stairs. Never had the flight seemed so long. In his impatience even the latch of his chamber door seemed to be obstinate. The envelope bore the post-mark, "G——," and on its face, in Irene's characteristic hand, he read "Marshal Dudley."

"Her answer!" he ejaculated, his heart in his mouth. No, he reflected, it could not be a reply to his confession, else she would not have addressed it to his assumed name. He stood motionless at a window and held the envelope in his hand, wondering what it contained, yet dreading to know. He turned the letter over, taking heart as he felt its thickness. If unfavorable, why had she used so much paper? Nervously he broke the seal. A blur came before his eyes. She had recognized his handwriting and returned his letter unopened.

Through all that long miserable day he did not leave his room. He turned a hundred times to look at the envelope she had directed. He sat listlessly at his window and looked out at the brown walls opposite, and at the people passing by. When night came he went out; he felt

11

as if he could hardly breathe indoors. He walked through the streets for hours—walked till the noise of hoofs and wheels was hushed. Then he went back to his room, as miserable as ever man was. Irene despised him. She would never give him a chance to ask forgiveness, she who had once given him her young heart so trustingly.

Several days passed. The few friends who saw him thought that he was going to be dangerously ill. One day, while brooding over the past summer, the thought came to him to write a novel depicting his own life-struggle between right and wrong and his final repentance and remorse. The idea filled him with exalted emotions. He would make it an artistically disguised confession of his whole vacillating career; he would show himself just as he had been and was. Irene should read it. She would then understand the depth of his repentance and might perhaps forgive him.

Filled with his new-born hope, he set to work. He wrote by day, by night; his very heart's blood seemed to drip from his pen. As days passed he grew paler and thinner; his eyes shone with a strange hectic light from the depths of their dark sockets. Friends who met him turned from him with pity in their hearts. Some thought his mind was going astray.

At last his work was done; the final page was written. On his way to his publishers, he had to stop several times to rest. Entering the office he came face to face with Mr. Princeton, one of the firm, and his warm friend, but the latter did not recognize him.

"Whom did you wish to see, sir?" Mr. Princeton asked.

"You, Mr. Princeton, if you please."

The old gentleman looked at him again, and fell back, astonished.

"My God, Morton! this can't be you!"

"Yes." And a smile that was almost repulsive came over Edgar's cadaverous features. "I have finished a book for you." He was running the tips of his ink-dyed fingers aimlessly over the package on his arm. "I intended to copy it again, but when I started to do so I— I found that there would be few, if any, changes to make. When I see the proofs I can attend to them."

"We shall read it and announce it at once, my dear boy," said the publisher, sympathetically. "We are having calls for a new book from you on all sides. But now, my poor dear fellow, you must go home and take a rest; you will be ill; you have worked too hard."

The next morning, as Edgar was sitting at his window gazing listlessly out into the street, a boy came to tell him that the publishers wanted to see him about his manuscript. A shiver ran over him. He replied that he would go at once. He was filled with misgivings. Had they found his work unworthy of publication? Could he, after all, in his condition of mind and body, have been able to do himself justice. His heart sank very low indeed; he began to fear that he had made a great mistake. The subject had interested him, of course, but could he have made it interesting to others?

"What is it, Mr. Princeton?" he asked, a few moments later, as he stood at the publisher's desk.

The old man rose, and putting his arm around Morton, led him silently into an adjoining room. Morton's heart was in his mouth. When they were seated side by side, Mr. Princeton said, huskily:

"My dear boy, I may not be infallible in my

judgment, but I think your story is the strongest piece of work of the kind ever written— ever written, I say. I read it last night, and could not put it down till finished. Old as I am, I cried over it. Two of our readers are looking over it together in the office now, and they are wildly enthusiastic. My boy, your fame and fortune are made. Your first book showed wonderful promise; this is perfectly grand. It has more purity of soul, more moral tone in it than anything I ever read."

Mr. Princeton felt his companion lean against him. He looked at his face.

He had swooned.

CHAPTER XV.

In her melancholy life Irene had but one desire—to help her father out of his financial troubles. She could think of little else, for she noticed the dear old face growing graver and sadder day by day.

" Papa, tell me about your debts," she said, one day, surprising a troubled look in his eyes; and she came and sat down by him at the cheerful wood fire.

He put his hand upon her head and with quivering fingers brushed back her hair from her forehead. The frown which had been fretting his brow all day vanished.

" Don't trouble your young head about me, pet," he said, smiling faintly. " We shall pull through somehow. All we need is five hundred dollars, and that will come somehow. I am not worthy to be the father of such a girl as you. I was always a poor manager, and here of late, I have been worse than ever."

She sat down on his knee, nestled into his arms, and closed his mouth with a tender kiss. Then she ran from the room to keep him from seeing the tears which were springing into her eyes.

She watched every mail with deep anxiety, hoping to hear that the publishers had accepted her novel. One day, when her father came home at noon, he said:

"Here is a bulky letter for you, my dear. It is addressed in a masculine hand and is from New York."

Her heart rose into her mouth. She held her breath, and was almost afraid to look at the letter. What if he had written? Mr. Stanton gave it to her. She did not touch it. It fell into her lap, and she sat, mute and motionless, looking at it with flashing eyes, her face paling, and her nostrils quivering. She had recognized Edgar Morton's handwriting. Presently she bit her lip and a slight angry flush came into her face. Then she sat up very erectly, and looked at her father.

"Papa," she said, in a tone of mingled excitement and enforced calmness—"Papa, you said once, after Mr. Dudley left, that he had

given you his address; do you remember
it?"

The old man, who had already recognized
the handwriting on the letter, looked at his
daughter with kindling eyes.

"Yes, pet," and as he gave her the address,
he dropped his head, flattering himself that
he appeared very unsuspecting.

"New York?" she repeated coldly; "surely
not New York?"

"Yes, New York," the moving light still in
his eyes. "I asked him again, to make sure,
for I thought he was going back to Boston,
but he repeated that it was New York. I suppose he decided to go there after he left us,
you know."

Irene went into her study. Pale and agi-
tated, she sat down at her desk, put the letter,
unopened, into a large envelope, sealed it carefully, addressed it, and sent it to the post-office
by Judas. Then she lowered her white face
upon the desk and remained there—as if in
deep sleep—till she heard the dinner-bell.
She rose, forced a bright look into her face,
and went to walk out to dinner with her father.
As she put her hand on his arm, she smiled and

told him playfully that he was the dearest man
in all the world. And all through the meal,
he, poor, kind father ! uninitiated, as men
always are, in the mysterious wiles of woman-
kind, believed that the letter he had brought
had chased the deepest of her cares away,
and was content.

Late one afternoon she stood on the veranda
watching the dead leaves twirl down to the
dying grass. The day was cloudy. She had
succeeded in making herself believe that her
heart had grown quite indifferent to the man
she had once loved so fondly. All she cared
for now, she told herself, was to succeed with
her writings. She had sent Judas for the mail,
and was waiting impatiently in expectation of
getting a letter from the publishers to whom
she had sent her novel. Success meant so
much to her—and to her father also—that she
felt that the rejection of her story would almost
kill her.

At last, through the paling of the front
fence, she saw the dwarf lazily sauntering up
the sidewalk. She put her hand to her heart,
and turned her back to the gate. Would he
bring her the letter she was so anxiously expect-

ing? She heard the click of the gate as it closed, but even then did not look round. Her eyes had a strange stare in their depths. So much did she dread disappointment that she did not look at the boy as he came clattering in his thick new shoes up the steps to her side.

"Miss Inie," he panted, with a broad grin, "I got suppen fer you."

She looked down at him. He was holding a package toward her.

"No letter?" she said, in a suppressed tone, and the old sickening feeling of disappointment came over her again.

She took the package, and, looking it over, saw in the upper left-hand corner, the words, "From Lang & Princeton, Publishers, New York."

Her manuscript returned!

Her heart stood still. She held the package before her for a moment. Then it dawned upon her dull, dead comprehension that Judas was eying her in silent astonishment, and pride came to her aid. She smiled, trying to hide her pain even from him, but her lips were as tense and chill as dead ones.

"It's nothing, Judas, thank you for going,"

said she, huskily, "I shall not forget you when Christmas comes; it is not far off now."

"Twenty-nine days, Miss Inie," cried the child, joyfully; "marster tell mammy so dis mawnin'. Miss Inie, does yer know is de marshal gwine ter 'low de boys ter pop fire-crackers in de street dis Chris'mus? Dey oon let um las' time, kase some um tetch off Mr. Martin's barn en stable."

"I hope so, Judas," the pale girl returned, smiling stonily.

She turned into the hall and went slowly back to her study. With a sigh she put the unopened package upon her desk and left the room.

"So ends my dream! It has lasted since I was a little child," she said, firmly. "I was mistaken. He was mistaken; or perhaps he only led me to believe in order to——" She paused, and her face became very white. "No, no," she went on, "he could not have been so despicable. I should go mad if that were added to it all. No, he thought as I did. I am sure of that—almost."

When her father returned an hour later he found her, seated in front of the sitting-room fire. He had made a long journey into the country to see an old friend from whom he had hoped to borrow some money to pay the debt that was threatening him with ruin. Irene read his failure in his face and in his slow motions as he took off his overcoat and hung it up. She saw, also, that he was dreading to speak of his fruitless effort as he sat down by her and spread his cold hands out to the fire. She thought it best to have the subject over with at once.

" You did not get what you went after, papa," she said, assuming a light tone ; " but don't let that worry you. You are too old and frail now to have trouble. Don't think about it." And she laid her hand caressingly on his knee.

He tried to reply, but choked a little and remained silent. Presently he rose, with a little twinkle of pleasure in his eyes.

" I forgot," said he, going to his overcoat and returning with a letter. " Here is something for you. I got it at the office this morning before I started to the country. I have been carrying it all day."

She took it, feeling the same sharp pang that had struck her on the veranda, for the

envelope's corner bore in printed letters, "Lang
& Princeton, Publishers, New York."

It was only the letter accompanying the
rejected manuscript which she had already
received, she thought, and she regretted that the
two had not arrived together. Her father's eyes
were upon her inquiringly, and she suddenly
faced a new fear. She had not told him of her
work, and her little plan to help him, and he
must not now suspect her great disappointment; it would make him more unhappy. She
dropped the letter into her lap, placed her interlocked hands upon it, and pretended to forget
it.

"Why don't you read it?" the old man
asked.

Then, to guard her secret, she rose with
deceptive jaunt and went to a window as if to
catch the light from the pale western sky.
Opening the letter, she purposely let the envelope fall to the floor, that he might see she
was reading. When she drew out the written
sheet a folded paper and a crisp pink slip were
disclosed. She looked at them with kindling
curiosity, for their import did not dawn upon
her. The letter ran :

" Dear Miss Stanton—

" We owe you apologies for our delay in reporting upon your MS. Several members of our staff have been away this fall, and so many manuscripts came during their absence that we were unable to give yours a reading till quite recently. Otherwise you would have heard from us at once, for we assure you yours is one of the finest and most remarkable novels we have been able to secure in years. As you say you are not familiar with the terms usually extended to authors by publishers, and as we hope to be favored with other work from you in the future, we have made an exception in your case, and you will find the terms of enclosed contract as liberal even as those allowed to well-established writers. We have not read anything in late years more touching and strong, or better finished, than your book. The only American work from the pen of a young writer which equals it is ' Evolved,' a novel which we have just issued, by Edgar Morton.

" In consideration of your present need of money, as mentioned in your letter, we are pleased to enclose our check for one thousand dollars, having decided to publish your work first as a serial in our magazine.   Later we will issue the story in book-form.   If the terms of the enclosed contract are satisfactory, please sign the same and return to us with your receipt for the check.   Thanking you for sending your first work to us, and hoping that we may soon have something more from your pen, we are

<blockquote>
" Very sincerely yours,
" Lang & Princeton."
</blockquote>

The papers in Irene's hand were quivering. She glanced at her father.   His back was turned to her, and he was looking steadily into the fire.   The news was almost too good to be true.   Then she bethought herself of the unopened package, and, full of delicious wonder, hastened to find it.

It was dark in her little study, and she lighted a lamp with trembling hands.   On opening the parcel she found a book of about the same bulk as the manuscript which she had sent to the publishers.   In gilt letters, on the Russian-leather cover, she read, " Evolved :   A Novel.   Edgar Morton."

She sank into a chair and looked once more

at the letter and the check, the blood slowly flowing into her cheeks. Then she bethought herself of her father, and, thrilling with inexpressible joy, she hastened to where he sat in the firelight. His hands were clasped over his mud-spattered knee, and a great weight of depression rested on him. She entered so softly that he did not hear her, and stood a little behind him, hesitating for a moment. Then she laid the check across the letter, and handed them to him over his shoulder. As he took them he looked up into her eyes in an absent-minded way, then he put on his spectacles and read them in the firelight. She was watching him very closely, her joyous heart in her mouth. She saw him start; a strange look of perplexity came over his face. He read the check again, and then looked up to her inquiringly.

"It is all for you, papa dear," she said, smiling through her tears. "I should not care for success but to help you. It has made me so happy!"

He seemed to comprehend. He tried to lift his eyes again to hers, but failed. His head dropped a trifle. The red glow of the fire shone through his straggling gray hairs,

the papers in his hands quivered pitifully.
His head sank still lower, and his shoulders
rose and fell significantly. Irene stole into the
dining-room and without a word of warning
threw her arms around her aunt's neck, who
was scolding old Del for having made the coffee
too weak. The elder woman kissed her niece
fondly, wondering the while what had hap-
pened, and yet not daring to ask.

At the tea-table, a moment later, Mr. Stanton's face was full of warmth. When he bowed
his head to ask the blessing in his usual way,
he failed. His lips moved mutely for a con-
secrated moment, then he raised his head and
said "Amen," and avoided Mrs. Livingston's
surprised gaze over the steaming coffee-pot.

Aunt Millie, as she brought in the dishes,
threw a wondering glance at the faces around the
table, and then went back to Uncle Tony, who
was toasting his shins over the kitchen fire, and
hungrily eyeing a pan of hot biscuits in the
stove.

"Suppen done happen ter marster, Tony,"
she said; "yer cayn't fool dis yer chicken.
I seed 'im many er year in en out but never
des zackly lak he look now. I do know it beat

me sho! He des set deh en let his coffee git col', en w'en Miss Inie is busy wid 'er eatin', he look lak he could eat 'er whole. En whut beat all, Miz Liverston seem 'bout ez much set back ez I is. Seem lak she ain't mek head nur tail out'n it."

Irene left the old people at the table, and went to get Edgar Morton's new novel. She thought that Lang & Princeton had sent it, because they had mentioned it in their letter: it did not occur to her that it might have come from some one else.

She was reading it in the sitting-room, her pretty feet pushed out toward the fire, when her aunt came in with an altered face and a melting mien. She stopped behind Irene's chair, and, bending back the girl's head, kissed her tenderly, very tenderly, on the lips. Mr. Stanton, who had taken a seat at the fire, pretended not to notice the show of affection between the two. He looked steadily at a black cat asleep on the hearthrug, and put down his hand to stroke it gently, making the animal pur and contract its claws in the soft woollen texture.

Mrs. Livingston sat down at the piano for the first time since Mrs. Stanton's death. It was a quaint old air that she played, and her fingers had grown stiff from want of practice, but the shadows on the walls appeared to dance undulatingly to the music, and the blended fire and lamplight seemed an enchanted veil that had fallen upon the room. And Irene sat upon a shrine before two old worshippers, and all unconscious of their wordless adoration read " Evolved." They watched her changing face with displeasure. They wanted to take the book from her, for its contents seemed to throw a damper upon her happiness. They heard her sigh more than once, and her eyes began to swim in unshed tears. Every page reminded Irene of the past summer, and of Marshal Dudley. The hero of the story seemed strangely to possess his soul. She could not lay the book down. It chained her every thought, roused her deepest emotions. She read on till late into the night. Her father retired, with a look of troubled perplexity in his face ; and when the clock struck twelve Mrs. Livingston came and gently laid her hand across the page.

" Darling, you must not read longer," she said ; " it will make you sick. See, the fire is dying down, and it is twelve o'clock."

"Twelve o'clock!" repeated Irene, as if in a dream. "Why, I did not know it was so late. Have I kept you waiting, aunt?"

"Oh, no; we are all so happy over your good fortune that we wanted to sit up longer to-night. God has been good to us, dear."

"This story is very interesting," said Irene, closing the book, and turning away with her aunt to go upstairs. "I could not drop it. Perhaps it interested me more particularly because it is by Edgar Morton, and was sent to me by the publishers who have been so good to me. Besides, I was once so silly as to think, from reading his other novel: 'Transgression,' that he was not at heart a really good man. I remember I told Mr.—Mr. Dudley that I felt that way; but this is so grand, so pure, that I see I wronged him."

The first thing after breakfast next morning Irene slipped away to her study to finish the book undisturbed. She bent over it and at once became as deeply absorbed as on the previous evening. A strange alternating feeling of elation and regret possessed her. Once she laid the book down, trembling as she confronted a strange question. In some things the hero was

so like Dudley! Then she remembered that
he had said he knew the author of "Transgression." Could Dudley have had anything to
do with writing the book? She smiled feebly at
the idea, and read on, her whole soul wrapped
up in the story. Just as she reached the
point where the hero confesses to the heiress
to whom he is engaged, that he loves another,
Mrs. Livingston came to ask some question
about a dress.

Irene lifted eyes which shone with light
from within, stared her aunt straight but
vacantly in the face, and then looked down
again, without a word, to the pages before her.
Mrs. Livingston looked at her scrutinizingly,
an expression of pain in her face, and turned
away.

The story was almost ended. The hero was
in abject despair. The girl he really loved had
driven him away, and refused to listen to him.
She returned all his letters unopened. There
were but a few more leaves to turn. Irene's
heart felt as if it were bursting. A veil of
tears was before her eyes. Then she noticed
that two of the remaining pages had been
carefully pasted together. Separating them

with a paper-knife, she found a thin piece of
paper covered with Marshal Dudley's writing.
Her features waxed stone-like; she could not
imagine what it meant. She read:

"I have sought this way of reaching you—
of trying to make you understand the fathom-
less depth of my love, the depth and burthen
of my woe. I am Edgar Morton. I assumed
the name of Dudley that I might pursue my
studies in the South without being known as
an author. As I have described the character of Alfred Morgan in 'Evolved', so was
mine. All my life I have been continually
wavering between right and wrong—rising
and falling between the exalted and the low.
Until I met you, I had never known the
supreme satisfaction of right-doing. I intended to tell you who I was, but after your
just criticism of 'Transgression' that day, I
did not have the courage to do it. Give me
one more chance. I would die to see you and
dear old G—— again. Will you not write me
a single line of forgiveness—you who are so
good, so generous to all? I have confessed
my love for you to the woman to whom I

was engaged, and she has released me and is, in fact, to be married to another. You have made me a better man than I ever hoped to be. I love you with all my soul and cannot live without you. Can you forgive me? May I come down to see you?

        "Devotedly yours,
          "EDGAR MORTON."

Irene closed the book. She was alone. The fire had died out. The day was tottering down the hillside of the world into the valley of night. The house was as still as an empty cathedral. She looked from a window, Morton's letter in her hands, her features in the grasp of contending impulses. The wind was blowing a drift of dry leaves against the doorsteps. Irene sighed and left the window. She sat down at her desk, took up her pen, and dipped it in the ink. But she did not begin to write, and the ink dried. Again and again she dipped the pen, only to have it dry in her inactive fingers.

Before her hung the sketch she had made from the cliff on the mountain. She remembered how she had sat there alone. She saw

him come down the winding path to join her.
The blood came into her face. She remembered how she had slipped and fallen—how
he had risked his life to save her! Her
face grew hot. She saw herself in his arms,
her face close to his, her hair blowing around
his neck. He had begged her to let him fall
and save herself. Could she refuse to forgive
that man? Her face grew tremulous with
emotion, tender with regrets. She dipped her
pen again, hurriedly wrote a couple of lines
and her name, and put them in an envelope.
Then she went out to Aunt Millie's cottage
and asked for Judas.

"He's down deh, at Miz Moore's house," replied Aunt Millie; and she looked in wonder at
her mistress's face. "Why, Miss Inie, I b'lieve
you is kotch de happy fever too, lak de res' er
um. I ain' nuver seed de lak yit. De good
ole time is back ergin sho; en it's so nigh
Chris'mus-time too—mighty good sign!"

Irene smiled and tripped down the walk to
Mrs. Moore's cottage. The door was open,
and Mrs. Moore, who was working within,
invited her to enter.

"Aunt Millie said that I could find Judas

here," she explained, as she entered the cottage door. " I wanted him to mail a letter for me. I wish it to leave to-night."

" Yer I is, Miss Inie ! " exclaimed the little black, from a dark corner, where he sat on the floor, shelling popcorn.

" You can finish the popcorn when you get back, Judas," said the woman, wiping her hands on her apron, and apologizing for the disorder of her house.

" Judas, I want you to be very careful with this letter," said Irene ; " you must not lose it."

" Yesum, yesum," promised the dwarf ; " I'll be mighty keerful, Miss Inie ; " and he brushed the chaff from his diminutive trousers, and, taking the letter, bounded away.

After sitting a while, listening to Mrs. Moore's talk about her domestic affairs, Irene rose to go. Just then she heard a little whimper from a waking infant on a bed in a corner of the room. She ran to it impulsively, took the little blue-eyed creature into her arms, and kissed it several times, making the while sweet motherly sounds, and praising its beauty. Mrs. Moore flushed red with pride.

"You are very good to notice her, Miss Irene," she said, tremulously; "and her dress is so dirty. I did not know that you were fond of children."

Irene's face reddened a little, and she pressed her warm cheek to the tiny white one. Then, without replying, she put the child into its mother's arms. The last reflex of day illumined her face and outlined her trim, supple figure as she tripped up the path past the negro cottages, restraining a light song which she had learned to sing when she was a happy school-girl.

Yule-tide flowed gently in. Christmas-day dawned gray and cloud-draped, but with it came a balmy breath from the south, which made the day as warm as spring. Early in the morning, guns began to boom from all sides of the town. Now and then loud yells rang out in the quiet streets. The sky reflected a great blaze, a barrel of tar was burning in an open space in the centre of the town; and half a dozen church bells began to ring out gleefully.

A score of black fists hammered upon the doors of the Stanton residence.

"Chris'mus gif', Marse Stanton! Chris'mus gif', Miss Inie! Christmas gif', Miz Liverson!" was shouted in a chorus that shook the walls.

"Christmas gift to you all!" cried Mr. Stanton, raising a window and putting out his head.

"We got yer, marster; we got yer; no use backin' out. We is kotch yer wid yo' eyes shet dis time sho!" said Tony, chuckling.

Then they joined other negroes that were passing by, and men, women, and children ran pell-mell to the houses of neighbors, repeating the same storm of raps and cries.

"Chrism'us gif' ter y' all! Chris'mus gif' ter everybody in dis yer house, ole en young! Glory fer Chris'mus!"

But by the time the whites had risen at the Stanton's, the servants were all back, huddled round the great kitchen fire, which Aunt Millie had made, waiting patiently for the sitting-room door to open. Experience had taught them what to expect. You might as well have told them that a stone tossed in air would not return to earth as that the members of the Stanton family would forget them on that day.

About eight o'clock a tiny bell rang in the sitting-room. Every black mortal stood on his feet. Even imperturbable Aunt Millie's eyes shone with expectancy, and she hastened to dry her hands on a dish-cloth and follow the others. They entered the sitting-room softly and took places round the walls in chairs which had been placed for them. For a moment after all were seated, a crackling fire, built upon a great Yule log which Tony had laid away to dry six months before, made the only noise that broke the stillness. The master, near whom sat Irene and her aunt, opened the big family Bible, read a chapter, and then motioned them all to kneel.

During the prayer many eyes peered cautiously through fingers that masked expectant faces. Judas dropped slowly down till he sat on the floor, so as to peer under the master's chair to see where the Christmas gifts were hidden. But the child had more faith than Thomas of old, for though he had not seen with his own eyes, his faith was as unshaken as a mountain of stone. The "Amen" came so suddenly that, in attempting to get up, with his hands still over his face, he bumped his

woolly head against his chair; and he stood,
looking very guilty, under Aunt Millie's re-
proving eyes.

"My foot went ter sleep," he said, senten-
tiously; "it tickles mighty funny yit. I hatter
set down on it so long while marster is pray."

"You des wait tell I git er hick'ry ter you,
young man," threatened Aunt Millie, in a low
tone; "I'll mek you think yo' foot ersleep—
cuttin' up sech oudacious shines yer on sech
er 'casion."

It was a happy throng which marched out
of the room a few moments later, exclaiming
in chorus: "Thankee, marster; thankee, Miss
Inie; thankee, Miz Liverson!" for they had
all received just such gifts as they most needed
and desired. Little Judas chuckled and
grinned profusely as he left with a new suit
of clothes, a pair of red-topped boots, and a
package of fireworks and candies.

On the afternoon of that day Edgar Morton
arrived in the town and walked over from the
hotel. Care and ill-health had marred the
youthful fullness of his features, but there was
a tremulous look of happiness in his eyes that

in a measure atoned for it. He saw no one on the lawn but Judas.

"Is Miss Irene at home?" he asked, approaching the boy, who was charging an ink-bottle with powder, and preparing to touch it off through a fuse.

" Yes, suh, I b'lieve she is," he said, failing to recognize that delightful acquaintance of his, who used to toss dimes and nickels into the air to see him scramble for them in the grass.

"Don't you know me, Judas?"

Judas eyed him intently for an instant, then he said:

"Well, suh! ef it ain't Marse Dudley, sho!"

Morton winced a little at the name, and waited patiently, with his eyes on the house, while Judas told him, as he held up a hand bound in blood-stained rags, that a white boy had invited him to shoot off a big "kickin' hoss-pistol, loaded ter de top wid powder en wet wads—wet, min' yer, en chawed tight. Did yer ever?

" Why, Marse Dudley," he went on, exposing the whites of his eyes comically—" why, suh, des ez soon ez dat thing go off I keeled over lak er dead jay-bird. I thought my

whole side is split off. Ef I'd des been er lill
bigger I'd er mash dat feller's snout tell it's
ez mushy ez er rotten cucumber. Mammy sez
powder is dangersome. You des listen fer dis
bottle w'en I git it fix."

In response to Morton's ring a little black
girl opened the door, and looked very much
astonished when she recognized him. He went
into the parlor, where a great fire was burning.
The yellow glow cast around the room made
the sultry day without seem veritable night
by contrast.

He did not sit down. His heart was beating
furiously ; it stood still as he recognized Irene's
light step on the stairs. She was quite pale,
but she looked unspeakably happy and beautiful, in her black gown, as she lingered for a
moment in the hall. In that moment he wondered if he could calmly meet the dear eyes that
had haunted him all during his absence. But
when she came toward him in the firelight,
and he saw the sweet blending of sympathy,
tenderness and joy in her features, his eyes
leapt to flame, and a thrill of ineffable delight ran through his veins.

She shyly held out her hand, but he took

her yielding form into his arms and pressed his
lips to hers.

The whistling of the wind outside and the
rattling of the windows was all that broke the
silence.

THE END.

BOOKS

From the Press of the Arena Publishing Company.

Salome Shepard, Reformer.

By HELEN M. WINSLOW. A New England story. Price: paper, 50 cents; cloth, $1.00.

The Law of Laws.

By S. B. WAIT. The author takes advance metaphysical grounds on the origin, nature, and destiny of the soul.

> "It is offered as a contribution to the thought of that unnumbered fraternity of spirit whose members are found wherever souls are sensitive to the impact of the truth and feel another's burden as their own."— *Author's Preface.*

256 pages; handsome cloth. Price, postpaid, $1.50.

Life. A Novel.

By WILLIAM W. WHEELER. A book of thrilling interest from cover to cover.

> In the form of a novel called "LIFE," William W. Wheeler has put before the public some of the clearest statements of logical ideas regarding humanity's present aspects, its inherent and manifest powers, and its future, that we have ever read. The book is strong, keen, powerful; running over with thought, so expressed as to clearly convey the author's ideas; everything is to the point, nothing superfluous—and for this it is specially admirable. — *The Boston Times.*

Price: paper, 50 cents; cloth, $1.00.

For sale by all booksellers. Sent postpaid upon receipt of the price.

Arena Publishing Company,

Copley Square,   BOSTON, MASS.

BOOKS

From the Press of the Arena Publishing Company.

COPLEY SQUARE SERIES.

I. Bond-Holders and Bread-Winners.

By S. S. KING, Esq., Kansas City, Kansas. The most power-ful book of the year. Its argument is irresistible. You should read it.

> President L. L. POLK, National F. A. and I. U., says: "It should be placed in the hands of every voter of this country."

Price, postpaid, 25 cents ; per hundred, $12.50.

II. Money, Land, and Transportation.

CONTENTS:

1. **A New Declaration of Rights.** *Hamlin Garland.*
2. **The Farmer, Investor, and the Railway.** *C. Wood Davis.*
3. **The Independent Party and Money at Cost.** *R. B. Hassell.*

Price, single copy, 25 cents ; per hundred, $10.

III. Industrial Freedom. The Triple Demand of Labor.

CONTENTS:

1. **The Money Question.** *Hon. John Davis.*
2. **The Sub-Treasury Plan.** *C. C. Post.*
3. **The Railroad Problem.** *C. Wood Davis and Ex-Gov. Lionel A. Sheldon.*

Price, single copy, 25 cents ; per hundred, $10.

For sale by all booksellers. Sent postpaid upon receipt of the price.

Arena Publishing Company,

Copley Square, BOSTON, MASS.

BOOKS

From the Press of the Arena Publishing Company.

Is This Your Son, My Lord?

By HELEN H. GARDENER. The most powerful novel written by an American. A terrible *expose* of conventional immorality and hypocrisy. Price: paper, 50 cents; cloth, $1.00.

Pray You, Sir, Whose Daughter?

By HELEN H. GARDENER. A brilliant novel of to-day, dealing with social purity and the "age of consent" laws. Price: paper, 50 cents; cloth, $1.00.

A Spoil of Office.

A novel. By HAMLIN GARLAND. The truest picture of Western life that has appeared in American fiction. Price: paper, 50 cents; cloth, $1.00.

Lessons Learned from Other Lives.

By B. O. FLOWER.

There are fourteen biographies in this volume, dealing with the lives of Seneca and Epictetus, the great Roman philosophers; Joan of Arc, the warrior maid; Henry Clay, the statesman; Edwin Booth and Joseph Jefferson, the actors; John Howard Payne, William Cullen Bryant, Edgar Allan Poe, Alice and Phœbe Cary, and John G. Whittier, the poets; Alfred Russell Wallace, the scientist; Victor Hugo, the many-sided man of genius.

"The book sparkles with literary jewels." — *Christian Leader*, Cincinnati, Ohio.

Price: paper, 50 cents; cloth. $1.00.

For sale by all booksellers. Sent postpaid upon receipt of the price.

Arena Publishing Company,

Copley Square, **BOSTON, MASS.**

BOOKS

From the Press of the Arena Publishing Company.

Along Shore with a Man of War.

By MARGUERITE DICKINS. A delightful story of travel, delightfully told, handsomely illustrated, and beautifully bound. Price, postpaid, $1.50.

Evolution.

Popular lectures by leading thinkers, delivered before the Brooklyn Ethical Association. This work is of inestimable value to the general reader who is interested in Evolution as applied to religious, scientific, and social themes. It is the joint work of a number of the foremost thinkers in America to-day. One volume, handsome cloth, illustrated, complete index. 408 pp. Price, postpaid, $2.00.

Sociology.

Popular lectures by eminent thinkers, delivered before the Brooklyn Ethical Association. This work is a companion volume to "Evolution," and presents the best thought of representative thinkers on social evolution. One volume, handsome cloth, with diagram and complete index. 412 pp. Price, postpaid, $2.00.

For sale by all booksellers. Sent postpaid upon receipt of the price.

Arena Publishing Company,

Copley Square,   BOSTON, MASS.

BOOKS

From the Press of the Arena Publishing Company.

Jason Edwards: An Average Man.

By HAMLIN GARLAND. A powerful and realistic story of to-day. Price: paper, 50 cents; cloth, $1.00.

Who Lies? An Interrogation.

By BLUM and ALEXANDER. A book that is well worth reading. Price: paper, 50 cents; cloth, $1.00.

Main Travelled Roads.

Six Mississippi Valley stories. By HAMLIN GARLAND.

"The sturdy spirit of true democracy runs through this book."— *Review of Reviews.*

Price: paper, 50 cents; cloth, $1.00.

Irrepressible Conflict Between Two World-Theories.

By Rev. MINOT J. SAVAGE. The most powerful presentation of Theistic Evolution *versus* Orthodoxy that has ever appeared. Price: paper, 50 cents; cloth, $1.00.

For sale by all booksellers. Sent postpaid upon receipt of the price.

Arena Publishing Company,

Copley Square,   BOSTON, MASS.